"I have a seri~~ous~~ ~~proposition for~~ you."

God, even after all these years of mutual dislike and loathing, even after he'd married another model, a woman a few years older than she was, whom she'd nevertheless considered her mentor and close friend, whom he'd had a child with, even after he'd blamed her for helping his marriage to Jacqueline combust, how could she still feel this giddy anticipation? When was she going to get over this...ridiculous fascination with Nasir?

"How interesting," Yana said, pouring her excitement on thick even as her belly twisted into a knot. Leaning toward him, she mock-whispered, "But my kind of propositions are not usually your... *forte.*"

Billion-Dollar Fairy Tales

Once upon a temptation...

Meet the Reddy sisters—Nush, Mira and Yana. As the granddaughters of tech tycoon Rao Reddy, their lives have been full of glitz and glamour. Until tragedy strikes and their beloved grandfather passes away. Amid their devastation, each girl finds a note, Rao's last gift for them to help them live out their dreams. But chasing their happiness won't be a smooth ride!

Nush has been in love with her longtime family friend and billionaire boss, Caio, for longer than she can remember. She's ready to move on... but then he proposes they have a convenient marriage!

Read Nush and Caio's story in
Marriage Bargain with Her Brazilian Boss

Mira and Aristos's marriage was purely for convenience, but Mira fled their powerfully real connection. Now...she's back with not one but two surprises!

Read Mira and Aristos's story in
The Reason for His Wife's Return

Yana and Nasir avoided the temptation of their connection once before, but now that they're bound together by a mutually beneficial deal, will the heat between them become too hot to ignore—or resist?

Read Yana and Nasir's story in
An Innocent's Deal with the Devil

All available now!

Tara Pammi

AN INNOCENT'S DEAL
WITH THE DEVIL

HARLEQUIN®
PRESENTS™

Recycling programs
for this product may
not exist in your area.

ISBN-13: 978-1-335-59228-6

An Innocent's Deal with the Devil

For questions and comments about the quality of this book,
please contact us at CustomerService@Harlequin.com.

Harlequin Enterprises ULC
22 Adelaide St. West, 41st Floor
Toronto, Ontario M5H 4E3, Canada
www.Harlequin.com

Printed in U.S.A.

Tara Pammi can't remember a moment when she wasn't lost in a book—especially a romance, which was much more exciting than a mathematics textbook at school. Years later, Tara's wild imagination and love for the written word revealed what she really wanted to do. Now she pairs alpha males who think they know everything with strong women who knock that theory and them off their feet!

Books by Tara Pammi

Harlequin Presents

Returning for His Unknown Son

Billion-Dollar Fairy Tales

Marriage Bargain with Her Brazilian Boss
The Reason for His Wife's Return

Born into Bollywood

Claiming His Bollywood Cinderella
The Surprise Bollywood Baby
The Secret She Kept in Bollywood

Once Upon a Temptation

The Flaw in His Marriage Plan

Signed, Sealed...Seduced

The Playboy's "I Do" Deal

Visit the Author Profile page at Harlequin.com for more titles.

CHAPTER ONE

SHE WAS NOT just broke. She was in a mountain of debt. And now that she was finally ready to admit her blunders and bawl her eyes out and beg him for help, the one man who'd loved her was gone.

Yana Reddy walked through the quiet, dark halls of her grandparents' house like a night wraith wandering through the dark woods from one of her favorite fantasy stories.

While her younger half sister, Nush, had always proclaimed her love of fairy tales, it was the much darker fantasy tales populated with demons and ghouls and djinns that drew Yana's interest. Especially one particular author she'd fallen in love with at a young age. Even then, her tastes had been drawn to the forbidden.

Now her grandfather leaving notes for his three granddaughters from beyond the grave appealed to her. She pulled the crisp folded letter out of its envelope and pushed it back in again without reading it, like she'd done a hundred times that day—the day they'd officially said goodbye to him.

Unlike both her half sisters, Mira and Nush, who'd burst into happy tears at one last note from their beloved Thaata, she knew the moment she'd seen her name written in that beautiful cursive script, that she wasn't going to read it.

Not yet.

Maybe not ever.

That would be her punishment. Plus, the possibility of a forever unclaimed present appealed to the contrarian in her. One last ploy to annoy Thaata.

A few hours ago the house had been full of extended family, friends and people who'd loved and respected her grandfather, who'd started a software company called OneTech, which his protege Caio Oliveira had turned into a billion-dollar venture.

Thaata had believed in second chances. Only Yana had never been able to use one to prove herself worthy like her sisters had done. To make him look at her with respect and love. Not frustrated resignation and the pain that he couldn't reach her.

Their alcoholic father had clearly preferred variety in his sexual partners for none of the sisters shared a mother, so Yana's grandparents had been the only responsible adults in their lives, and had essentially raised the three girls.

But all through her childhood and adolescence, Yana had resented them for it. Had chosen, in her early teens, to go and live with her flighty, unreliable, beautiful mother, Diana, instead of what she'd considered to be the much stricter regime of her grandparents.

By the time she'd realized the irreparable damage Diana had done to her, it had been too late. She'd trusted a woman who had, in return, emptied out all of Yana's bank accounts to pay for a cleverly disguised gambling habit.

Worse, in the last few months, Diana had ruined Yana's credit by borrowing off her credit cards when she'd refused to carry on funding her extravagant spending.

Closing the door to her grandparents' bedroom behind her, Yana fought the grief that had kept bubbling up like lava. If she let it out, it would burn her through, leaving nothing but ashes. She walked around, trailing her fingers over Thaata's things—a worn-out leather diary on his nightstand, a biography title on his desk and a picture of her, Mira and Nush with him.

It had been taken during one glorious summer where Yana hadn't fought with him or her grandmother, when Diana had gone to live with her brand-new second husband.

How could you have made such a wrong choice? she wanted to scream at her teenage self. How could she have chosen to live with her mother, who'd shown her nothing but neglect and abuse, over the grandparents who'd only wanted the best for her?

A woman who'd eagerly asked Yana about the *assets* that Thaata might have left her only a day after his death. Yana didn't have to wait for the reading of the will to tell Diana that whatever assets Thaata might have left her would be all tied up so that she couldn't touch them for a very long time. A witness to Yana and her grandfather's arguments more than once, Diana had believed it.

She'd left instantly, leaving Yana with a crippling debt. Just…breezed out of her life with barely a goodbye.

Almost nearing thirty now, Yana's modeling contracts were coming few and far between. As she didn't want to be a model for the rest of her life, she'd already given up on most of the networking necessary to stay current. She thought again about the new career—a work in progress for some years—she'd hoped would take shape before her life had fractured into tiny fragments.

For a second she considered asking Mira or Nush to help her sort out the mess her life had become. But she couldn't. And not just because they were finally moving forward in their own lives with men they loved.

Hitting rock bottom had cleared up one thing for Yana—she'd fix her life by herself. It was the only way to restore her own faith in herself.

Grabbing the keys of Thaata's vintage car and one of his cigars from a secret compartment in his dresser, she tiptoed back to her room.

Rummaging through her closet, she grabbed a black leather corset top and skinny jeans and got dressed. Pushing her feet into stilettos, she tied her hair into a high ponytail, slapped on mascara and lip gloss without looking at the mirror and rushed to the garage.

The crisp night made goose bumps rise up on her skin as she drove with the windows rolled down. With the engine humming sweetly and the scent of the cigar smoke filling her nostrils, she felt a measure of peace, for the first time in weeks.

Running away again, a voice very much like Thaata's taunted, but Yana refused to listen to it now just as she'd done when he'd been alive.

Yana knew who the man was the moment the double doors of the secluded VIP lounge of the night club opened. He stood framed by the archway bathed in beams of purple lighting.

She knew even though it was dark and quiet.

She knew before that distinctive gait brought him to the chaise longue over which she'd draped herself, having fought off three different men who'd wanted to take her home.

She knew because she'd always possessed a weird extra sense when it came to *him*.

A Yana's stupid-for-this-man sense.

A basic, lizard-brain *wanting* that screamed she was prey even though he'd never played predator. A let's-ditch-any-self-respect-and-make-a-play-for-him urge.

Nasir Hadeed.

World-famous fantasy author, current political strategist and retired investigative journalist, reclusive billionaire and most important of all— her stepbrother for just four years.

They'd only ever spent a few months under the same roof out of the four years his father had been married to Diana. During the time when she'd transformed from a gangly, awkward fifteen to a leggy, brazen, stupidly confident nineteen, who'd imagined herself to be a tempting seductress.

Already, Nasir had been successful, renowned and respected in literary circles and the political world as a just-retired war-zone correspondent.

Twelve years older than she was, he'd not only been incisively brilliant in ways Yana couldn't comprehend, but also effortlessly suave and stunning with a roguish glint in his eyes that the world didn't see. His brilliant, award-winning tracts on war zones and world issues hadn't captured her heart, though.

It had been the fantasy novels he'd written, garnering worldwide acclaim that had thoroughly captivated her. Those brief months she'd spent with him had been in a different universe in which he hadn't loathed her. An alternate, upside-down timeline.

He'd indulged her overlong, extravagant breakfasts at the palatial mansion that had been his father's house in Monaco—when she'd demanded to know why a loathed character had to be redeemed or a favorite one had met her demise—with a dispassionate fondness and that dark smile. As if she were a stray dog he'd pat on the head and throw a few morsels of affection at.

But thanks to her behavior on her nineteenth birthday, when he'd returned from the incident overseas that had given him all those scars, he'd written her off forever.

How Yana wished she possessed one of those time stones he'd written about in one of his novels. So many wrong and questionable and self-defeating decisions she could erase with one turn of the stone. Especially when it came to Thaata and him.

Two men—two of the most important men in her life who'd influenced her, made her want to be more than who she was. One of them, her grandfather, was forever gone now thinking the worst of her, and one was determined to think the worst of her forever. She wiped at a stray tear that flew into her hair, donning the superficial persona that had become like a second skin now.

Because if Nasir pitied her, she'd just fall apart.

One signal from Nasir to the nearly invisible bartender and bright lights illuminated the dark corner. Immediately, he moved to block the glare that made Yana blink gritty eyes.

Shards of light traced the blade-sharp cheekbones, the hollows beneath and the wide, thin-lipped mouth. And the scar that bisected his upper lip and zigzagged through his left cheek—the remnant of a near-fatal knife wound that had changed the trajectory of his life. And hers, in a way.

Awareness pressed down on her as he took her in with that quiet intensity. She'd never understood how there could be such intense energy between them when they detested each other.

"Hello, Yana."

A full body shiver overtook her and still, she lay there, stupidly gaping at him, gathering her armor, which had already been battered by grief and loss. "Am I in hell, then?"

In response, he shrugged off his jacket and draped it over her mostly exposed chest and bare shoulders. She'd always marveled at how cruel and dispassionate Nasir's kindness could be. Still, she couldn't sit up. Couldn't get her heart to stop thundering away in her ears. "Go away, Nasir. I'm in full party-girl mode and as we both know, you're lethally allergic to that."

It was like craving the warmth of the sun but spending years trying to figure out how to ignore its existence in the sky.

Of course, the hateful man sat down on the coffee table, cornering her. Despite the dark, even with her stomach hurting because she'd barely eaten anything the whole day, even with her head in a weird limbo of grief and self-directed rage, warmth unspooled low in her belly at the familiar scent of him.

Bergamot and sandalwood—it was as if a chemist had experimented and figured out the perfect combination of scents that provoked all of her sexual fantasies and then doused Nasir Hadeed in it.

Two minutes in his company and Yana wanted to kiss the man senseless and curse him to whatever hell would torment him the most. The only constants in her life were her abiding love for her sisters and this mad obsession…for Nasir.

She took a puff on her cigar, blew out a ring like a photographer friend of hers had taught her. Not her fault that Nasir chose to sit right in that space.

Shadows created by the interplay of darkness and light gave his face a saturnine cast. As if those stark features needed to be tarred with any more harshness. Light, amber-colored eyes, deep-set and invasively perceptive, met hers. The large beak of his nose—which should have rendered him ugly but instead made him look intellectual—made it effortlessly easy for him to look down on her.

"How are you, Yana?"

She took another puff of the cigar. "How did you know where to find me?"

"One of your staff followed you here and called me."

Raising a brow, she went for insouciance that she didn't feel in the least. "Keeping tabs on your favorite supermodel, you naughty man?"

Something flitted in and out of those thickly fringed eyes, too fast for her to catch it. "I was nearby when you tore out of the garage as if a demon was chasing you."

"I didn't realize I was so important to you that you'd come all this way to pay your respects to my grandfather," she said, going on the offensive.

There was no other way to act around him. Shields up one hundred percent and donning titanium armor, like the prickly heroine in her favorite sci-fi show. Also based on a novel this very man had written.

Seriously, her obsession with him had no chance of petering out when she gorged herself on every word he'd ever written—novels and articles and newsletters and political treatises—like a wanton glutton.

"Clearly, it was a self-indulgent fantasy to imagine I'd find you behaving like a responsible, normal adult in the throes of grief." The cigar that she'd barely taken two puffs of was roughly yanked away from her lips and put out with a pinch of fingers that should have burned him but drew not even a quiet hiss. "That's a disgusting habit and a lethal one, too."

"Did you miss me so much that you came all this way to harass me, Nasir? No one else to look down on and feel better about yourself?"

"I came here because I need you."

Yana sat up with the force of a coiled spring that had been stretched too far back, for far too long. Her head swam, the reason anything from starvation to the special kind of dizziness only he could cause. "Huh! The world is upside down today, I guess. Or I'm traveling through parallel universes like Uzma does," she said, mentioning the intrepid heroine of his latest novel. Plucking her phone from her jeweled designer clutch, she opened the camera app and thrust it in his face. "Care to repeat that so that I can record it?"

Silence lingered, full of his infinite patience and her childish taunts.

"Fine." She straightened her posture on the chaise, tucking her knees away from his. They were both tall people and in the tight space of his legs, her awareness was on steroids.

She tried to not linger on the way his black trousers bunched at his thighs, or the way the white shirt open to his chest drew her gaze to the swirls of hair on dark olive skin. Or the large platinum-faced dial of his watch on a corded wrist. Or the long, bare fingers that had once—only once—lingered on her jaw with something almost bordering on tenderness.

"I have a serious proposition for you."

God, even after all these years of mutual dislike and loathing, even after he'd married another model, a woman a few years older than she was, whom she'd nevertheless considered her mentor and close friend, whom he'd had a child with, even after he'd blamed her for helping his marriage to Jacqueline combust, how could she still feel this giddy anticipation? When was she going to get over this...ridiculous fascination with him?

"How interesting," she said, pouring her excitement on thick even as her belly twisted into a knot. Leaning toward him, she mock-whispered, "But my kind of propositions are not usually your...*forte*."

A muscle jumped in his jaw, the scar twisting with the action. He thrust a hand through that thick, wavy hair he usually kept military short. "Oh, believe me. Having found you in a nightclub two days after your grandfather's death, smoking a cigar, looking like you do... I'm questioning my common sense in even being here."

"Ahh...now, that's the guy I know and love to loathe." A tinkling laugh escaped her. "Come, Nasir. You might be a diplomat in the biggest political circles and the hottest bachelor on the planet but it's the lowest denominator of you I get, no? Let's not try something new today, of all days. I've had enough shocks, thank you very much."

Remorse flashed through those usually inscrutable eyes. "I'm sorry for your loss, Yana. I know that grief takes different forms—"

"You don't know anything about my relationship with Thaata."

"Fair enough."

Irritation and hunger and something more danced across Yana's skin as she studied him.

"It's about Zara."

His daughter. Her facade fell away like snakeskin. She reached for his hands but pulled away at the last minute. "Why the hell couldn't you have opened with that instead of insulting me?"

"Your worry about her is real." He sounded stunned.

"And you're an ass."

Feeling caged, her breaths coming shallow, she stood up. Her foot had fallen asleep on her, forcing her to grab him to keep her balance.

His white linen shirt proved no barrier to the firm muscles underneath and the heat coming off him. Under her fingers, his abdomen clenched.

The sensation of his hot, hard body under her touch stung her palm. His grip on her tightened as she tried to yank herself away. "Damn it, Yana! Stay still." The tips of his fingers pressed into her bare arm; one corded arm wrapped around her waist. It was too much contact and hyperventilation wasn't far away. "Or you'll ruin that pretty face and any hope of—"

"What's wrong with Zara?"

Now that she'd managed her overreaction to his proximity, she could see the exhaustion beneath his calm. It made the light, slightly raised tissue of his scar stand out in stark contrast to the rest of his skin. Worry and fatigue carved deep grooves around his wide mouth.

An answering pang vibrated within her chest.

"She's fine, physically. But losing her mother at that young age, even one as mostly absent as Jacqueline was…the doctors are saying she's not adjusting well to the loss." His Adam's apple moved up and down as he swallowed. "We've tried everything. It has been…painful to see a bubbly, extroverted child like her withdraw to that extent. I'm at a loss as to how to help her."

"Children are much more resilient than we give them credit for. With support, Zara will get over losing Jacqueline."

"Have you gotten over your mom's neglectful, bordering on abusive behavior toward you?"

Something hot and oily bellowed under her skin. "That's none of your business."

"I'm just saying Zara shouldn't have to go through this alone."

"How is she alone when she has you?"

"I've tried my damnedest to get close to her. Don't pretend as if you don't know how things are between us. How Jacqueline messed everything up. How she tried to cut me off from my own daughter."

"I don't want to talk about Jacqueline."

"I don't, either." He rubbed a hand over his face. "This is about Zara. Not you, not me and definitely not her mother. She lights up when you text her or video call her. She talks for hours about your chats, your emails, the cards you send her from all over the world. That collection of keychains you've given her over the years… Every single one is worn down for how much she plays with them." A shuddering sigh made his chest rise and fall. "She keeps asking for you, Yana."

Yana jerked away from him, wobbled again and braced herself against the back of a dark leather sofa. Shame coiled tight in her chest. "I'm sorry I haven't been to visit her recently."

Damn it, how could she have forgotten all the promises she'd made to Zara when Jacqueline had fallen ill? Why had she gotten involved when she had such an abysmal record at handling expectations? What about being the child of two absent, neglectful, narcissistic parents equipped her to handle a fragile child? "Between losing my grandparents only months apart and work—" and keeping her head afloat while her mother robbed her blind "—I… I've been scattered."

"Nothing new in how you live your life, then, huh?"

His criticism stung hard and deep.

She loved Zara. Loved her despite the fact that Jacqueline had used Yana's tumultuous feelings for Nasir to feel better about her crumbling marriage. Despite the fact that he loathed the very sight of Yana.

Under the guise of fixing her hair, she dabbed at the tears prickling behind her eyes. Her failure rubbed her hollow.

She had failed Zara. After vowing to herself that she wouldn't let the little girl feel alone in the world like she'd once felt.

The vague headache that had been hunting her all day returned with a vengeance, making her light-headed. Or was it the fact that she'd skipped lunch and dinner and her sugar levels were falling fast? "No, nothing new."

A soft curse escaped his mouth.

Nasir never cursed and if she was feeling normal, she'd have recognized it for the win it was. Suddenly, she became aware of the heat of his body at her back and her dizziness intensified. His fingers landed on her shoulders, the rough pads deliciously abrasive against her bare skin.

"I'm sorry. I came to ask you for help. For a favor. To…beg you if I need to. And yet, I can't seem to stop insulting you."

"Nothing new in how you talk to me either,

then, huh?" Yana glared at him and sighed. "I want to see her. I do. Zara's important to me, one of the few important people in my life. But..." She rubbed at her pounding temples. "Right now things are impossible to get away from."

"That's where the proposition part comes in."

"Not necessary. I love Zara as if she were..." She bit her lip, heat flooding her cheeks.

My own, she'd been about to say. Which was laughable even in thought because she was the last person who should be responsible for a young girl. She couldn't even manage her own life without sinking into debt and self-rage.

Nasir's amber-colored eyes gleamed. "And yet, you don't act like she is. She's seen you once since Jacqueline died."

"I just told you I've been busy with shoots and—"

"I've heard whispers that you're completely broke. If that's true, I really don't care how it happened. I'll pay all your debts and pay you whatever sum you demand on top if you come spend the next three months with Zara."

"No."

Her answer reverberated in the quiet around them, the darkness amplifying it.

No, I don't want to be anywhere near you.

No, I don't want to spend three months under the same roof as you.

No, I finally have enough self-preservation to

not cut myself down just because you hate me. No, no, no.

Even if that meant breaking her promise to Zara.

"I know you have no way out of the financial hole you've dug yourself—"

"No."

"Because your modeling contracts are drying up—"

"No."

"So my bet is that any assets you have will be seized soon and—"

"No."

"Damn it, Yana! You need this as much as Zara needs you."

"No," Yana repeated, even as the word continued to ring in her ears and her vision was blurring and fading and she felt nauseated and dizzy and…

"Yana…look at me. Yana! What the hell have you done to yourself now, you…"

He's really beautiful. The errant thought dropped into Yana's fading consciousness.

Nasir grabbed her and pulled her to him, and she could finally see the amber flecks in his eyes and the long, curved lashes casting shadows onto razor-sharp cheekbones. He was looking at her as if he didn't loathe her. As if he was actually worried about her. As if he…

No, she couldn't spend three months with the man she'd loved for half her life.

Not that she loved him anymore. *Not at all.* The tightness in her chest was only an echo of what she'd once felt for him.

Yana fainted and in the flash of a second before she lost consciousness, she had the disturbingly pitiful thought that Nasir had caught her. That he hadn't let her fall to the ground.

CHAPTER TWO

NASIR HADEED WALKED the perimeter of the VIP lounge like a caged predator as the young doctor that had been dragged from the exotic restaurant downstairs examined Yana. He glanced at his watch for the hundredth time in the last half hour, a powerless ire simmering under his skin.

She'd remained unconscious for three and a half minutes. It had, however, felt like a hundred eternities. His heart hadn't yet calmed down from its rapid pounding rhythm.

Despite his long career in war-torn zones and some of the most dangerous places in the world, despite having tasted the loss of a woman he'd loved once that had forever calcified his heart, he'd never been so terrified as when Yana had folded into his arms like a cardboard doll. Amidst her litany of *nos*.

The saving grace had been that he'd shouted for his bodyguard/assistant. Ahmed had had the presence of mind to immediately commandeer a doctor.

Nasir had rubbed her arms up and down as soon as he'd carried her to the chaise longue. Even with her light brown hair hanging in a limp, messy ponytail, her lips chapped and even bleeding in a couple of places for she had the habit of worrying her lips with her teeth, her face a sickly sheen of white, she was still the most stunningly beautiful woman he'd ever seen.

Worse, not an hour in her company and he was cursing her recklessness, his own decisions that had led him to need her, and the universe all in one go.

And his weakness when it came to her, too, for he hadn't been able to stop running his fingers over the jut of those legendary cheekbones and the sharp, elongated tip of her signature nose that had skyrocketed her to fame at the tender age of sixteen.

Once she'd recovered consciousness, he'd moved to the far end of the cavernous lounge. To give her privacy and to get himself under control. *Ya, Allah*, what was wrong with him?

He'd chased her halfway around the world to this damned nightclub because he needed her for his daughter. And yet, all he'd done was insult her, over and over again.

Where was the diplomat the world lauded? Where was the responsible father of a five-year-old?

I always get the lowest denominator of you...

If only she knew how close to the vulgar truth she was. How she inspired and invoked and ignited his basest instincts. When she taunted him. When those gorgeous brown eyes landed near his mouth and skidded away. When she simply fluttered about in the locus of his own existence.

Her soft whispers as she spoke to the young doctor, the quiet but husky chuckle, the trembling shoulders…everything about her called to him.

If only he could see the beautiful, vapid, vain teen she'd suddenly turned into one summer, he'd have no problem dealing with her.

His disastrous marriage to Jacqueline Yusuf—a sophisticated model and businesswoman he'd once considered his equal in every way—had completely cured him of the stupidity of trusting his judgment when it came to women.

But Yana…had always been indefinably stubborn and refused to be slotted into any one box.

He couldn't look at her and not remember the fifteen-year-old who'd shyly hero-worshipped him the first time he'd visited his father and his new wife. Or the one who'd begged for his autograph on a first edition. Or the passionate, sweet teenager who'd yelled and cried when he'd killed off her favorite character, or the hug she'd given him with an endearing smile on her suddenly stunning face when he'd brought that favorite character of hers back to life in the next novel.

He couldn't not see the nineteen-year-old who'd

shocked him by walking through his room ditching pieces of clothing on the way to his bed, boldly declaring that she loved him with all of her heart, body and soul.

Or the girl who'd lied to her mother that Nasir had kissed her. Or the woman who'd looked as if she'd been dealt a staggering blow when Jacqueline, her friend and mentor, had introduced him as her fiancé. Or the woman who'd barely met his eyes when she'd stood by Jacqueline's side when they'd gotten married.

Or the woman who'd lied more than once to help hide Jacqueline's many affairs from him. Or the woman who'd stayed by Jacqueline's bedside for the last few weeks during her battle with cancer.

Or the woman who had miraculously managed to carve a place for herself in his young daughter's heart. Or the woman he'd touched in tenderness after Jacqueline had died, not a few minutes before his lawyers had discovered that Jacqueline had been preparing to sue him for solo custody of Zara, and Yana would have been the character witness to prove his negligence toward his daughter.

And yet, he'd learned, only after Jacqueline had died, how Yana had spent hours entertaining Zara, watching her, cooking for her, reading to her while Jacqueline was supposed to have been looking after her, how much attention she'd bestowed on his daughter when it should have been her mother doing that, how many times Jacqueline had dropped her off with Yana.

Yana Auntie this, Yana Auntie that... It was all his five-year-old girl would speak of. Just when Nasir had written Yana off entirely, the blasted woman revealed a new, complex dimension to herself that had dragged him back under her spell.

She loathed him and yet, she was capable of genuinely loving his child. What was he supposed to make of her? If only this ridiculous attraction he'd fought for so long would fade.

But he needed her and damn it, he needed Yana well again and ready to spar with him.

He needed her to not look like a lost waif, one hard breath away from falling apart. He needed her to fight him tooth and nail so that he didn't have to feel guilty about how he'd talked to her tonight.

She *had* just lost her grandparents—the only responsible adults she'd known in her life. And he'd done nothing but insult her and minimize her very real grief.

He'd never met another woman who provoked such extreme reactions in him. Not even Fatima—the woman he'd loved a lifetime ago—had tied him up in knots like Yana did.

From the tendrils of tenderness that had swamped him as he'd held her, to the rage that she didn't care enough about her own health. Even back then, he'd only learned of her diabetes when she'd gone into shock due to low sugar levels. It had been reckless and naive and foolish at sixteen. Now, almost thirteen years later… Had she still no sense of self-preservation?

What if he hadn't been there to catch her when she'd fainted and force feed her the bar of chocolate when she'd recovered consciousness? What if no one knew her whereabouts and she'd lain there for hours, going into shock? What if he'd had to inform his child that her Yana Auntie had taken seriously ill, too?

And he was inviting this…train wreck, this selfish, infuriatingly stubborn woman into his precious little girl's life.

Into his own life.

Into his space—his haven, which he allowed no one into.

It was like issuing an invitation to chaos and mayhem and sheer madness to reside in his house, in his head, in his heart.

"Here, sir," said Ahmed, stalling his walk, a bottle of water in his hand.

Nasir shook his head, too tired to reprimand the older man for addressing him using the honorific.

"Is Ms. Reddy okay, do you think?"

On cue, Yana laughed, leaning toward the young doctor.

He *wasn't* jealous of her attention toward the damned doctor, or her laughter or whatever it was she was saying to him. *He wasn't.*

"It was a miracle you caught her, Inshallah," Ahmed continued, unaware of his employer's roiling emotions. "Or she might have really hurt herself."

Nasir grunted and restarted his perambulations of the lounge, cutting closer and closer to where the doctor was now entering her phone number into his own cell phone. If he gritted his teeth any tighter, he was going to need dental work.

"Did the doctor say what caused the faint?" Ahmed asked.

"She probably forgot to eat." Nasir cleared his throat. "She's diabetic."

"I remember. Anything else you need from me?"

"No, get some sleep. We'll leave for London first thing tomorrow morning."

"Ms. Reddy has agreed to spend time with Zara baby, then?" Ahmed inquired, all polite affability.

Yana's multiple *nos* echoed inside Nasir's head like a chant. She hadn't simply refused him. No, she'd looked horrified—as if he'd invited her to sacrifice herself at some demon's altar.

He usually encouraged that impression of himself in most people, including his extended family and friends. That she saw him as some kind of autocratic, unfeeling beast grated, though.

"Sir?"

"No, she hasn't agreed." He bit out the words. "But she will. Even if it means I have to—"

"I know that you and Ms. Reddy don't see eye to eye, but I will not support kidnapping the young woman, sir. Even for Zara baby's sake."

Nasir laughed, the tension in his muscles relaxing for the first time in days. His bodyguard's strait-laced morality and hero complex never ceased to amaze him. "Things are going to be hard enough dealing with her, Ahmed. She doesn't need you as her champion."

"Beg your pardon, sir, but your father taught me that everyone deserves a champion. Ms. Reddy does, too. Especially since I've never seen you treat anyone with the kind of..." Ahmed broke off, then cast him an arch look that communicated everything he didn't say. "Have you forgotten how much your mother loathes Ms. Reddy?"

"She'll understand that Zara needs her," Nasir said, but even he didn't believe it. His mother's reaction to his bringing Yana home was a bridge he'd cross when he came to it.

"I just think bringing Zara baby to her could've been easier," Ahmed added with infinite patience.

"And let her drag Zara around like unwanted luggage just like Jacqueline did? Let my five-year-old daughter be exposed to alcohol and drugs and parties and toxic behaviors like her mother did? Should I also expose her to all the lurid gossip about her mother and her lovers that's still flying around even after all these months?"

"You're holding your wife's past mistakes against Ms. Reddy. I've never known you to be so…cruel." Ahmed sighed. "It *is* a hard situation. But if Ms. Reddy says she cannot make it, then she must have a good reason. I have seen her with Zara baby and she adores her, just as much as the little girl adores Ms. Reddy."

The conviction in Ahmed's voice only fortified his own. "Don't worry, Ahmed. I won't make you a party to this. You can catch a different flight." His jaw tight, Nasir stared at the woman who was sure to cause him untold problems once he was in his house. "But by kidnapping or some other way, she's coming home with me."

"Who's kidnapping whom?" Yana asked behind him.

Nasir turned around to find the young doctor glancing up adoringly at her, his arm propping her up. "Everything okay, Doc?" he asked, wishing he could laser the man's arm off with his vision.

"I'm fine," muttered the irritated voice next to him.

Whatever the doctor saw in Nasir's face, he replied hurriedly, "Ms. Reddy's vitals are all good. Just exhaustion brought on by weakness."

"Glucose levels?"

"Normal. The chocolate bar you fed her helped stabilize her. She just needs lots of rest, hydration and proper meals."

"Ahmed," Nasir said, somehow holding on to the last thread of his patience.

His bodyguard escorted the reluctant, dazed doctor out the door while he was still shaking his cell phone in Yana's direction in the universal sign of "call me."

Finally, Nasir turned his attention to her.

Yana stood leaning against another high-backed lounger, her fingers fiddling with the jacket he'd draped over her. *His* jacket.

It hung on her shoulders, the thick collar drawing his gaze to the smooth skin between her small breasts and the one button holding it closed farther down. The tie holding her hair together had fallen off and now the golden-brown waves fell past her shoulders, the edges curling up.

"Don't treat me like an idiot," she bit out, all huskiness gone.

She still looked pale to him, but at least the fight was back in her. "Don't act like one, then."

"Just because you've caught me out at a bad time doesn't mean you get to look down that arrogant beak of a nose at me."

"You fainted, Yana," he said, gritting his teeth

again. "And didn't respond for three and a half minutes."

Even the obvious fright in his tone had no effect on her.

"It's been a horrible few weeks. No, months. Seeing you just made it worse. I told you but you didn't listen."

When she wobbled, Nasir caught her at the waist. She fell into him with a soft thud, a quiet, enraged growl escaping her mouth. He felt her anger, her grief, her resignation, as if they were his own. Felt the force of her aversion to him.

"I hate you," she whispered, almost to herself. "I hate that you're the one who found me when I'm at my lowest."

Nasir let them wash over him, hoping the venom and rage in her words would dilute his own awareness. Her face close to his, her warm breath feathered over his jaw. Then there was the prick of her fingernails into his forearm. The wildcat was doing that on purpose and yet, the sensation only made his arousal sharper.

This was how it would be every minute between them—she cursing at him and he…would be in a constant state of arousal. It was funny, really, how they'd come full circle. She loathed him now and he couldn't be near her without his body betraying him like a damned teenager.

For a man who'd seen that heaven and hell could exist side by side on this very earth, maybe this was just punishment for his cruelty toward her. When she'd been nineteen and had needed firm handling and kind words and not his blistering wrath. When she'd been his bride's maid of honor at their wedding, Jacki's nurse at her bedside, a grief-stricken best friend with his child sobbing in her arms.

For a second he indulged the idea of telling her what her nearness did to him. Of shocking her as she constantly did him.

Would she be disgusted by his near-constant desire for her? Would she call him a roaring hypocrite as he deserved? Or would she simply count him as one among the scores of lecherous men that hit on her?

Slowly, feeling as if he'd run a marathon with no victory at the end, he tugged the neckline of her jacket higher.

"Can you please stop manhandling me? I'm all sweaty and gross. And why the hell did you cut open my top?"

"You were hyperventilating even before you fainted." He'd thanked the dim lighting of the lounge as the leather of her corset top had splayed open under the sharpness of his penknife. He didn't need more pictures of her naked perfection in his head. "That damned thing was so tight it's a miracle you could breathe."

Earlier she'd been too cold. Now her skin was warm as he held her up. The indent of her tiny waist, the slight flare of her hips, the jut of her hip bone, the smooth warmth of her skin…everything about her was fragile in his fingers.

"Let me go," she demanded.

"You'll kiss the floor the second I do," he said, holding himself rigid and stiff. Even with the aroma of cigar and the leather of the nightclub clinging to her, she smelled good.

It had been too long since he'd held a woman like this. Since he'd had sex. Since he'd worked out the pent-up frustrations of his body instead of engaging his mind.

Learning of Jacqueline's affairs had put him off relationships. Swiping left or right or whatever the hell side he was supposed to, casual dating or sex with strangers…he hadn't been fond of it in his twenties. At forty-two, the very idea of taking some strange woman to his bed made him want to hurl. And yet, every inch of his body was buzzing with an electric hum now.

Ironic that the one woman who made him react this way at the most innocent of contacts was someone he could never have. Even for a casual fling.

"Escort me to a cab, then."

"No."

"Have Ahmed drive me home, then."

"No. And for God's sake, stop arguing with me just for the heck of it."

"Or what?" she said, thrusting her face into his with a belligerence that got his blood pumping.

"Don't push me, Yana. We'll go to my hotel suite, where you'll eat, sleep for however many hours your body needs and then, in the morning, we'll finish our discussion."

"I don't want to spend another minute around you." She stepped back from him, palms raised. "If I have a heart attack next, it will all be your fault, Nasir."

He'd had enough. "You can screech and scream like a banshee for all I care. I'm not letting you out of my sight anytime soon."

Without batting an eyelid, he picked her up and threw her over his shoulder, fireman style. God, she weighed so little that he didn't even breathe hard, though it had been a while since his job demanded something so physical.

To his eternal surprise, she fell quiet. And he knew it was because she was on the last reserves of her energy. The chocolate bar would only prop her up for a while. Her quiet resignation rid him of any guilt that he was railroading her when she was feeling this weak.

She needed looking after as much as his five-year-old did, at least for a little while. Resolve renewed, he forged through the screaming throes of the nightclub.

Barely a few minutes later he crossed the foyer, then pushed the button for the elevator with

Ahmed at his back. Thank God he'd booked a full suite at the same hotel. Still, they'd caught more than one curious hotel guest's attention. More than one eager paparazzo's prurient gaze.

But at least he had her now.

CHAPTER THREE

THE UNIVERSE WAS really cruel, Yana thought, as
the man she'd taught herself to hate—and, oh,
how easy he made it for her—placed her on his
bed with a tenderness that stemmed from all the
wrong reasons.

She rolled away from him using energy she
didn't have and instantly regretted the impulse.
It was *his* bed she was rolling in; his suite he'd
brought her to. That heady cocktail of clean sweat
and his signature scent clung to the sheets.

If she closed her eyes, she could still feel the
hard dig of his shoulder over her belly, his muscled back smushing her breasts, his corded forearm at the tops of her thighs, holding her in place.
Even more shocking was his sudden devolution
from the veneer of the starchy, uptight, no-public-
display gentleman he'd always shown the world.

*Who was this Nasir who had no control over
his words or his actions?*

Slowly, she sat up, cataloging the exhaustion
sweeping through her. She was hungry. Tired.

Her mouth felt dry and gritty. But she hadn't had a fainting spell in years. Not that Nasir would believe her.

The stress of the past few weeks, her new medication and the fact that she hadn't eaten all day... they were excuses, however valid. She'd let herself drift into chaos again.

But better Nasir who found her than Mira or Nush or God forbid Caio—who took protective instincts to a whole other level. Her sisters would've been very upset at how close to burnout she'd edged. They'd have blamed themselves and that was a vicious cycle she'd never enter again with loved ones.

At least with Nasir, she'd had a lifetime of dealing with his contempt.

But if there was one thing they had in common, it was the stubborn tenacity once they decided on a course.

She saw it in his face now, in the tight set of his jaw. In the edgy energy that imbued his usually elegant movements. He'd decided that Zara needed her and he was determined to drag her with him. But as much as she adored Zara, how could she be a stabilizing influence on her when her own life was only two streets away from utter mayhem?

Brow furrowed, Nasir approached the bed as if she were a wild animal he hoped to not provoke.

Yana splayed her arms over the thick headboard behind her and straightened. "I won't bite, Nasir." When his jaw tightened, she grinned. "I mean, I know you're much too conventional to enjoy something so...outside the box."

"Good to see your usual...spark back. As for what I enjoy..." His gaze skidded toward her mouth and away so fast that she wasn't sure if she'd imagined it. "Just because I don't advertise my desires for all the world to see doesn't mean they're all vanilla."

A shiver of pleasure ran down her spine—keenly felt after the miserable past few months. Damn, but the man could play.

With each step he took toward her, fantasies she'd buried years ago roared back to life. Done in pale pinks and warm yellows, the luxury suite amplified the stark, forbidding sensuality of the man. There had always been something almost ascetic about him. And like in the stories of celestial women who seduced sages, Yana had always imagined herself to be the one who broke through his reserve.

Coming to a stop at the foot of the bed, he rolled a bottle of water toward her on the silk sheets. She emptied it in a matter of seconds, wiping the water that dripped down her chin with the back of her hand. All the while, his gaze seared like a physical touch.

"One would think you'd take better care of your body seeing how it's your only livelihood."

She held her automatic response by the last frayed thread of self-control. Her dreams for the future, her hopes for a different career... He hadn't won the privilege of hearing about them. On the contrary, she wouldn't be surprised if he mocked her for having them in the first place. Curling her lip, she said, "One would think you'd have more capacity for empathy and understanding given you've seen the worst of the world."

His mouth flinched.

Had she wounded him? Was that even possible for a mere mortal like her?

"You're right. I have been overly judgmental when it comes to you. But that shouldn't preclude you from—"

"Please, Nasir. Try to understand. I cannot come with you." She let him hear her frustration, let him see her powerlessness in granting him this wish.

Amber-brown eyes searched hers. "Of course, you can. It's a choice you make to put someone else's needs, a child's needs, before your own." Hands tucked into his trouser pockets, he studied her with dispassionate intensity. "Tell me what I can do to sweeten the pot."

She raised a brow, calling on all the haughtiness cameras had taught her to fake most of her life. "How pedestrian and predictable of you,

Nasir. Like every other man, you think you can buy me. Even my grandfather couldn't rise above bribes to make me behave."

"We both know you're in a financial hole. I'm giving you an easy way out." He rubbed a finger over his brow. "I admit I'm surprised you're not running toward me to snatch my hand off."

"Or you underestimate my loathing for sharing a roof with you."

Their gazes met and held. Memories swirled across the distance between them.

Long, dark nights spent in Jacqueline's Paris apartment watching over her as her death drew nearer. In those few weeks she'd spent at her friend's side, an intimacy of sorts had developed between Nasir and her. A byproduct of being so close to mortality, no doubt.

It had been more insidious than physical attraction, more dangerous. An intense curiosity in his eyes—as if he meant to peel away her armor and see beneath. As if, for the first time in their history, he found her interesting.

She'd even seen a flash of admiration in his eyes, and if she wasn't careful, she'd begin chasing it all over again. Like her mother was forever chasing the impossible win at the gambling tables. Like her dad with his alcoholic binges.

Addiction was in her genes. Only her drug of choice was this man's approval. And desire. And respect. And want. And her own need to bring him to his distinguished knees.

Not a week after Jacqueline's death, he'd turned on her. Accused her of conspiring with his late wife to separate Zara from him permanently. Accused her of cozying up to him even as she'd planned to betray him again. He'd consigned the worst motives to her actions and written her off as a backstabbing bitch, without giving her a single chance to defend herself.

His consequent cruelty was a shield Yana couldn't let go of.

"If I was wrong about you—"

"If?" she bit out. "Is it any wonder that I find rotting in penury more appealing than being saved by you?" She let out a huff, breaking eye contact and adjusting the oversize jacket around her shoulders. As if all of this was nothing but a nuisance she could shrug off. "Why couldn't you have just brought Zara to me?"

"Because she's already gone through too much upheaval in the last few months."

"Fine. You can oversee our visit together, looking down your beaky nose and holding me up to your impossible standards. I'd love to spend time with her here."

"Or you could be smart and just accept my help. It's not like you have a thousand other offers."

"Arrogant of you to assume that I don't have

people who'd dig me out of my financial hole as you call it. All I have to do is ask."

"Like who?"

"Like my sisters, who are both independently wealthy," she blurted out, hating his arrogant assumption that she'd been abandoned by one and all. That no one found her worthy just because he didn't. "Like Caio, who's my grandfather's right-hand man and my brother-in-law, and the new CEO of OneTech. Like Aristos, my other billionaire brother-in-law."

"And yet, you haven't confided in any of them, have you? Why is that, I wonder?"

Every minute with him was a danger to her persona of shallow supermodel. "How do you know you haven't caught me right before I did that? As tacky as I can be, even I know not to ask for handouts just two days after my grandfather passed away."

"I don't believe you. I think you hate the thought of asking them for help. Of letting them see how spectacularly you've failed in managing your life. Especially when one of your sisters is a doctor and the other's a...coding genius. After all, you have that stubborn pride to contend with."

Dismay filled her at how clearly he could see through to her deepest wound. But then, no one else knew her flaws as well as he did.

She was saved from responding when his phone gave a series of loud pings. His frown went into scowl territory with each swipe of his fingers.

She pushed onto her knees. "Is it Zara? What's wrong?"

"Some imbecile snapped a pic of us going into the elevator." A pithy curse flew from his mouth. "It's clear it's you and me." His scowl changed direction. "You don't care?"

She shrugged, examining his reaction. His privacy was sacrosanct to him. No one even knew where his permanent residence was. "That cute doctor, can we make sure he doesn't leak that I fainted?"

A shrewd glint dawned in his eyes. "You don't care about being linked with me but you don't want anyone to know you fainted?"

She blurted out before she thought better, "I don't want my sisters to know."

"A hint of a rumor about you and me just months after Jacqueline's death…"

"Everything that mattered to me is…already gone. So please, keep your threats of destruction to yourself."

It was not some dramatic threat or a bait for pity.

The resignation in her eyes burned Nasir with its honest edge. And for a second, he felt the most overwhelming urge to save her. From herself, if required.

God, he was as arrogant and egotistical as she

called him. "Not even if Zara were to hear of that kind of gossip about her Yana Auntie and her father?"

"She's only five." She jerked her head up, her golden hair spreading around her face as if she were a lioness shaking out her mane. "She wouldn't hear such...lurid gossip."

"And yet, she knows the name of every one of her *uncles* who visited her mama on photoshoots at work. She's aware that her mama was fobbing her off on you even before she was gone. She's confused and heartbroken, Yana."

Her curse rattled in the silence between them. She looked stricken and yet she rallied. "I'm not an easy fix you can use when you're overwhelmed and then throw away like some dirty Band-Aid when you're done. You threw me out of her life, Nasir. You told me to never return."

"So you'll punish Zara for my mistakes?"

"I'm not." She pressed a hand to her chest as if it physically hurt. "There's bad blood between us. It won't be long before she catches on to it. That's more confusion you're dumping on her."

"Then we'll start afresh with a clean slate."

She laughed then and it wasn't just mockery. The glint of tears in her eyes, the bitter twist to her mouth, spoke eloquently. "Hell has more chance of freezing over before you'll see me as anything more than—"

"So this is about your ego, then?" Frustration

and a powerless feeling burst out of Nasir. That he was being a beast to Yana was unforgivable. But that his past actions should now so adversely affect Zara, too, made him sick to his stomach. That he had forever calcified his heart as an unhealthy coping mechanism for an early loss in life, resulting in his worry that he wouldn't be able to connect with his own daughter, was a constant niggle at the back of his head.

"That I rejected your seduction attempt all those years ago? That I lost my temper over your continued lies about Jacqueline's affairs? That I'm telling you to your face that you're reckless and irresponsible and that you should get your life under control after you fainted in my arms?" he said, unraveling under the onslaught of a perfect storm of worries. "You're so insecure about one rejection ten years ago that you would abandon a child you claim to love when she needs you the most? Are you still just as desperate as you were back then for my approval?"

He couldn't bear to look at Yana's stricken face at his harsh words. He couldn't swallow the bitter lump in his throat that said he was no better a parent for Zara than Jacqueline had ever been.

"I don't want anything from you." Her whisper could have been a shout.

"Whether you accept my incentives or not is moot now. I know how to get you on the plane."

Large brown eyes searched his.

"I'll leak news of your debt to your sisters."

"You wouldn't."

"I will do anything to make Zara smile again," he said, grabbing the jacket he'd discarded earlier. "To not repeat the mistakes I've already made. So yes, I would tell the world that the incomparable Yana Reddy is so deep in debt that she can't even afford her own medication. That her team has jumped ship. Your sisters will pity you and—"

"You're a bastard."

"You know I am. So why sound so surprised?"

"And how do you know I won't fill Zara's mind with lies against you?" He didn't miss the cornered look on her face. A bitter smile pinched her mouth. "You've given me enough material over the years."

Some uncivilized part of him only she brought out wanted to growl like some wild animal at the threat. He was still fixing all the damage Jacqueline had caused by filling his daughter's tender heart with horrible lies about his apathy as a father. Still fixing his own blunders. For Yana to threaten him…

Nasir made himself take a deep breath. Forced himself to go with his instinct, to listen to his heart and his gut, instead of the more rational facts and fears. "I don't know that for certain," he said, the words coming more easily than he'd have imagined. Coming from some place he'd shut down a long time ago. "But I do know that however much you loathe me, you care deeply about Zara."

It was the dig about her wanting approval from Nasir that stuck like a craw in Yana's throat.

His words had cut her open as if he'd taken a scalpel to her skin. But examined again, out of his infuriating and overwhelming presence, as the blistering-hot water pounded out the soreness in her muscles that always accompanied her fainting spells, Yana acknowledged that it was the very truth that she'd spent years running from.

She'd always chased approval and validation—from her mother, from her grandparents, from her career, from Jacqueline. And she'd sought it in the most harmful, chaotic, childish ways possible.

For years, she'd wished she'd been smart and self-sufficient and self-composed like her older sister Mira. Then Nush had come into their lives and she'd wished she were full of hope and love and magic like her little sister was. Not forgetting that genius brain of hers.

Yana had always wished she were someone else. Someone more grounded, someone cleverer, someone more easygoing, someone less chaotic, someone healthier… The list of things she wasn't yet wanted to be was as long as the number of thugs Diana owed money to.

Even as Yana desperately wanted to be seen and appreciated and loved for herself at the same time.

Talk about confusing her little brain.

What Nasir was wrong about, though—and how she'd have liked to tell him that to his face— was that she'd sought his approval all those years ago with her pathetic seduction attempt. Or that she'd offered herself as some kind of cheap bargain. Or that she'd wreaked some sort of petty revenge afterward because he'd dented her ego.

As the hot water restored her sense and composure, she saw the root of her obsession with the blasted man.

Nasir was one of three people—her sisters Mira and Nush being the other two—who'd given her approval without her having to earn it with good behavior or better grades or by making restitutions because she'd ruined her mother's career simply by being born.

He hadn't judged her for being her mother's daughter or criticized her for being her chaotic, messy self, or mocked her for following him around with puppy-dog eyes anytime he'd visited. The four years she'd spent under the same roof as his father, the few months Nasir had joined them in between assignments and visits to his mother, he'd been unflinchingly kind to her.

Already making her name in modeling, Yana had been exposed to men and women wanting things from her. Her mother wanted the fame and fortune she'd lost by giving birth to Yana at a young age. Her alcoholic, mostly absent father wanted forgiveness in his rare moments of sobriety. How could she forgive someone who held no significance in her life except as a sperm donor?

The simple acceptance she'd received from an experienced, worldly man like Nasir had been like standing in sunbeams. Giving her the thing she'd craved most, he'd made her feel worthy of it.

There was magic in such unconditional acceptance.

She'd fallen for him with all the passion and intensity of first love, ready to sacrifice everything at his feet, follow him around the world with her heart in her eyes. Hence her pathetic seduction attempt. Just thinking of it now made her cringe in the shower.

And when he'd inevitably rejected her, with such brutal, cutting words that she'd forever lost not only her self-esteem but also his trust, she'd shattered. When her mother had found her running back to her room, tears running down her cheeks, Yana had lied to her that he'd kissed her.

Letting out a feral groan, Yana pressed her forehead to the pristine tile of the wall. It had been the stupidest trick she'd ever played in her life. In one stroke, with one foolish lie told out of the fear of making Diana angry, she'd made Nasir loathe her.

It was the same way she'd behaved with Thaata,

too. The more she'd wanted her grandfather's approval, the more she'd acted against her own self-interests, against her own well-being.

Never again. Never again would she let her self-worth be decided by anyone else. Not her mother. Not her grandfather. And definitely not Nasir.

Stepping out of the shower, Yana wiped the moisture from the large mirror and stared at her reflection. A smile broke through the worried twist of her mouth. She'd been in that chaotic, self-damaging place before and she'd clawed her way out of it. This time there was the added motivation of ensuring a five-year-old's well-being and happiness.

A girl just like her, wanting nothing but love from the adults around her. A chance for Yana to make sure Zara's life was different from what her own had been. She'd give the little girl all the attention and affection she'd always craved from Jacqueline, like Yana had craved from Diana.

And just maybe this three-month stint with Nasir and Zara was the universe throwing her a bone. She needed a place to recoup the loss she'd sustained, recover from her mother's betrayal and plan how to get her life back on the right path. On a different path. A path chosen by her and her alone.

She'd do it all without letting herself be swallowed up by the man who'd made her believe in herself a long time ago.

CHAPTER FOUR

It was a month later that Yana found herself aboard Nasir's private jet on the way to one of the tiny islands that made up Bali, after her last modeling shoot for a while. She hadn't wanted to keep him waiting once she'd agreed to his proposition, but it was impossible for her to just check out of her world for three months at a moment's notice, just because he demanded it. When she'd presented him with the various demands on her schedule, he'd agreed that she couldn't leave with him readily enough. But of course, she should've known that he wouldn't simply take her at her word.

As if things weren't confusing enough, he'd stayed with her, followed her wherever work took her, staying at the same penthouse suite at the same luxury hotel when she'd returned for Nush and Caio's wedding. The picture of them together in that elevator had run in an online gossip rag, which had eventually come to Mira's notice.

Yana had given her sister a sanitized version of

their fight and their subsequent agreement. Ever the practical and strategic Reddy sister, Mira had given Yana the best advice.

Treat it as a job. Be professional.

While Yana could see the simple yet profound wisdom in it, barely an hour since they'd taken off, she'd found it hard to implement.

Tapping her fingers on the armrest of her seat now, she studied the understated elegance of the aircraft's interior. Thanks to her modeling career, she'd traveled all over the world, to exotic destinations, no less. But her mode of transport hadn't always been this luxurious. Still, she could catalog the minor differences from when she'd traveled in such a cocoon of luxury.

The aircraft was state-of-the-art, but like Nasir, there was a quiet, industrial-type elegance to it rather than the flashy extravagance that most rich men she knew exemplified. Neither did she doubt that it was an efficient mode of transport for a man who traveled all over the Middle East and South Asia, instead of being a status symbol.

She'd had a month of him trailing her like a shadow, showing up at her shoots and events and even at her meetings with all manner of people, but Yana was still nowhere near used to his presence.

For the first time since she'd known him, she was going to get an exclusive glimpse into his very private life. When he and Jacqueline had been married, all the parties and gatherings that Jacqueline had hosted, even as a couple, had been at her apartment in Paris, or in New York.

Yana had even overheard a fight between them when he'd refused to open up his estate—wherever it was—for one of Jacqueline's "outrageous, drunken soirees" as he'd called them.

"You're jumpy and fidgety. Is there something you require?"

Straightening her pink satin jacket with exaggerated care, Yana counted to twenty before she turned to face him. For the past hour, she'd tried to treat him as part of the very elegant, luxurious background. It shouldn't have been hard with his long nose buried in the documents in front of him.

"Is the fidgeting and jumpiness bothering you?" she asked, with a saccharine sweetness that made even her teeth ache.

If only she could continue to ignore his magnetic presence. But it was like ignoring the sun while orbiting him in the sky.

"No." His answer came so reluctantly that Yana laughed.

"Lies."

"Okay, fine, yes. It bothers me. Do you need something?"

"No."

He returned his attention to putting away the documents in front of him.

Yana studied his profile, drawn as ever to it. His hair had grown long enough to curl thickly over his brow and reach past the nape of his neck. Dark circles hugged his eyes and there was a gauntness to his features that made his cheekbones stand out.

As she watched, he shrugged off his jacket, undid the platinum links at his cuffs and rolled back the sleeves of the white shirt, revealing strong forearms covered in dark hair. Her gaze leaped to his fingers undoing the buttons at his throat, eager anticipation fizzing through her.

The plain, platinum face of his watch—Jacqueline's gift on their second anniversary—was a much-required reminder to stop mooning over him.

Pulling off the glasses that gave him a serious, sexy professor vibe, he let that perceptive gaze rest on her. He didn't do an inventory of her. But she knew that he had noted every little detail about her, from her dyed strawberry blond hair to the deep V of her top.

A shiver ran down her spine. Suddenly, she wished she'd tried to nap, or at least pretended to have fallen asleep for the duration of the flight. "You didn't have to wait for me to join you."

"I promised Zara I'd bring you back with me, no matter when I returned this time. I couldn't take any more chances of disappointing her."

His tone was, for once, affable. And yet,

whether it was habit or some other defensive instinct, she felt the prick of his distrust. Took long, deep breaths through her nose, reminding herself that one of her own ground rules for this trip was that she'd be polite. No losing her temper, no riling him up and definitely no staring at him like a lost puppy, salivating with her tongue out and begging for a cuddle.

"I promised you I'd be there. I don't break my commitments."

"As that is something I'm not aware of, it made sense to stay and make sure."

"Do you have to turn everything into a character assassination?" she said, instantly regretting the combative words.

Why couldn't she just let it be? He was trying to be polite, trying to put that whole clean-slate nonsense into play. Acting as if they were nothing more than two strangers who'd shared and lost a common friend.

His long, rattling sigh told her she'd completely missed the mark. "The stakes are very high for me. Can we agree on that?"

She nodded, heat streaking her cheeks at his gentle tone.

"Good. Let's say it has nothing to do with you and your character and everything to do with my own shortcomings."

Picking at a loose thread on her cuff, she gave him another nod.

He was worried about how to reconnect with Zara after all the damage his marriage, and Jacqueline's lies and his own aversion to engage in a fight, had caused the little girl. It was etched into his features.

"I have some conditions," she said, deciding to steer the conversation to a necessary topic. Maybe that was even the best way to act, moving forward. Ignore the little blips of her temper, the squeaks her heart made whenever he was near.

He raised a brow at the sudden shift away from their argument. "Conditions? Isn't that something you should've discussed with me before you got on the plane?"

"You might have no faith in me, but I decided to show some in you. Even though…" She shook her head, cutting off that line of thought. "I just believed that you would be amenable to whatever I asked for so that these three months with Zara, *for Zara*, can pass with the least amount of aggression between us."

A long finger rubbed over his temple, even as one side of his mouth curled up. "You have given this a lot of thought."

"I've decided to treat this like any other contract. Professionally. I mean, I *have* had a lot of experience dealing with arrogant, egotistical, petulant men, who think they are a gift to the world. So why not draw from my almost fourteen years of experience?"

His reluctant smile turned into a full-fledged one. The sudden flash of his even white teeth and the deep groove it dug on one side of his face... She barely buried the sigh that wanted to leave her lips. God, the man's gorgeousness was lethal when he smiled like that.

"So what are they?"

"What are what?" she said, stuck in that sticky place.

His smile deepened. "The conditions you have for me?"

"Oh, yeah," she said, making a big show of pulling out her notepad from her giant clutch and opening to the right page. She had no doubt that a full-blown blush was painting her cheeks and lowered her head to hide the evidence. "You already took care of my debts. That was my first condition."

"Ahmed dealt with all that mess. He decided it wouldn't do for me to know all the gory details."

She looked up, surprise and relief rushing through her. Though she had a feeling it hadn't been Ahmed's decision so much as Nasir's. Which meant his belief that *she* had accrued that immense debt was being propagated further. And she needed that barrier between them, needed him to think she was reckless with every area of her life. "Remind me to thank Ahmed."

She looked down at her list and hesitated. A month ago she'd wanted to never set eyes on her mother again. To completely wash her hands of her. After this last betrayal, she'd thought herself incapable of caring the smallest amount about Diana.

And yet, over the past few weeks of having a clear goal and vision for her own life, of talking to Zara over video calls, of watching her sisters move on in their lives, she'd realized it wasn't in her to just walk away. To close her heart off. To abandon her mother when gambling was a mental illness.

What if Diana needed a fresh chance like Yana was getting from Nasir, albeit at a high price? Would she ever be happy if Diana wasn't also in a good place?

Her decision was driven not just by common sense but compassion and a sense of duty, too. Breaking away from toxic patterns, suddenly felt like it was within her reach. She could move forward with her own life then. But of course, she needed help. First, to gain a spot in that clinic she'd researched; second, to be able to pay for it; and third, to convince Diana to give it a try.

She'd decided to add the first two to Nasir's list.

"I need a recommendation for a rehab clinic. I've done my research and found one that's nestled in the Swiss Alps, but it's expensive and very exclusive. They usually only take people based on recommendations. From big shots like you."

His gaze immediately latched on to hers. "Rehab?"

"Yep. I've decided to tackle the bull by the horns, so to speak. For my gambling," she added, her throat dry over the lie.

Instead of seeing relief or even the self-righteous "I knew it" that she'd expected, a thoughtful look entered his eyes. "I'm glad you decided to seek professional help. Is it that bad, though?"

There was a tenderness to his voice that her brain wanted to cling to. Or was it her stupid heart? "How about we leave it to me to be the judge of that," she said tersely, because she didn't want him to probe.

"Of course, you're the judge," he added in a kind tone.

She sighed. Every dialog between them felt charged. Or perhaps she was making it so. "Some of us develop unhealthy, damaging coping mechanisms to deal with life." She wasn't addicted to gambling but she was addicted to something else, all right. "Not all of us are perfect with iron-clad control like you."

His mouth twisted with bitterness. "Not only am I far from perfect, but I'm only realizing now how *my* unhealthy coping mechanisms have hurt others. At least you're self-aware. I have been deliriously, arrogantly oblivious of my own failings."

Now it was she who wanted to probe. That

wanted to dig and dig until he was fully revealed and unraveled in front of her. That he'd hurt Jacqueline with his inability to love her was common knowledge between them. And yet, he'd never seemed to mind much before. She'd never seen a single hole in his convictions and beliefs about how he'd conducted his life.

Instead of giving full rein to that fascinated part of her, she forced herself to look down at her notepad.

"I will personally speak to someone on the board of administration," he said into the building silence. "Just let me know the timeline."

She nodded, running her finger down her scribbled list. "The next few things are not that big of a deal. I'm charging you twenty million euros for the three months. I'd prefer a bunch of chaperones as a buffer while I spend time with Zara and…"

His laughter was loud, booming around in the intimate space, pinging all over her skin. She looked up and lost her breath.

Head thrown back, muscles of his neck clenched tight, he was a study in masculine beauty. Attraction and desire tugged at her, a hook under her belly button pulling her closer, urging her to touch that smile, to taste that smile. Damn, she had it bad.

"What's so funny?" She went for irritation to hide her helpless attraction.

It was several minutes before he sobered up. "You are one expensive nanny, aren't you?"

A smile twitched at the corner of her lips. "Well, I guess I am. And please, before you come out with insults that I should be doing this out of the goodness of my heart, out of my love for Zara, don't. That's the price of me spending time under the same roof with you. Knowing that you will be overseeing everything I say, judging me, and…" It was hard to stay detached or antagonistic toward him when he looked at her with that smile stretching his sensuous lips.

"Fine. Agreed. You will have enough money at the end of three months. And believe me, we will have chaperones galore."

She turned a page on her notepad, gathering the courage to ask the most important question.

"Is that it?"

"I want Zara to spend one month out of every year with me going forward. It could be two periods of two weeks or four different weeks. I want that written into a contract."

"No."

Neither of them was surprised by his instant, biting answer.

The surge of rage and something else—a sharp helplessness, in her expression—told Nasir he'd given her the answer based on the rules and rationale that drove him. Had he been too quick to reply without thinking it over?

She tapped a pink nail incessantly over the table. "That one condition is non-negotiable. If you don't agree, I'll turn around and leave the second this plane lands." Every word was enunciated with a staggering conviction behind it.

"You're springing this on me at the last minute," he said, pushing for time.

Her brown gaze was pure challenge. "My relationship with Zara needs to exist outside of my relationship or lack thereof with you, Nasir. That's what adults should do. Put their differences, their egos, aside, for the sake of a child. I don't know what the future or the aftermath of these three months—" she said, laughing, with no actual humor in the sound "—is going to look like. This way, I'm ensuring that regardless of what happens between you and me, Zara always has me in her life. And not just as some patch-up you bring in when things get bad."

For the first time in his life, Nasir was speechless. Golden hair flying around her face as she bit out each word, Yana looked like a lioness defending her cub. "You're a natural at this, despite the fact both your parents neglected you."

She tilted her chin. Whatever fragility he had seen that first evening at the nightclub was all gone now. "It makes me even more empathetic to Zara's plight. She's just a child. No child should have to starve for attention or affection. Or get lost in adults' mind games." She played with the ends of her hair, her thrust delivered with an efficient, but impersonal bluntness he was coming to appreciate about her. He couldn't even get mad because she was right; Zara had gotten lost among his and Jacqueline's conflicts. "As for Diana messing up…" Her throat moved hard. "I've realized there have been good things in my life, too. It's on me whether I move forward with gratitude or bitterness."

"You sound very wise," he said.

"You sound shocked," she retorted with a cutting smile.

Clearly, in the past month she had returned to some sort of routine. He hadn't missed the fact, seeing he'd shadowed her wherever she went. Meals, regular exercise and medication on time, he could see the changes in her face. That gaunt, lost waif look was gone, leaving her effervescently beautiful.

He liked her like this—full of passion and conviction. Suddenly, he realized he had seen her like this before. Before she'd entered the modeling world as a far too naive and impressionable girl with only her mother's greedy, grasping behavior as a guide. Forced to grow up too fast. Acting out in the form of reckless, paparazzi-attracting, almost orchestrated publicity stunts.

There was a contentment to her now that he found extremely satisfying and that in turn was disconcerting, to say the least. He didn't want to be invested in Yana's happiness or well-being. Or only so far as it affected her relationship with Zara. God, that made him sound like an utter bastard.

"You look different," he said, unable to help himself.

She scrunched her nose, and even that twitch was sexy. "Good different?"

"Good different, yes." He didn't miss the hungry expectation in her eyes for more, but refused to cater to it. It was better if they behaved like polite strangers.

"Maybe the fact that—" she giggled, moving her hands in an arc toward him, encompassing the aircraft and the notepad, and everything else, her gestures getting wilder and more expansive with each passing second "—I'm making you pay through the nose is the cause of the change?"

"A small price to pay, then. Your happiness is quite the halo around you."

She gave him a regal nod in response. Then she studied her fingernails, going for that casual vibe that she never could quite pull off. "I think sometimes we have to hit our lowest point to see that things aren't as bad as we thought, that they can still be fixed."

He returned her somber nod, marveling at how deeply her words reached inside him. He'd been at that lowest point once. But unlike dreaming on a different vision as Yana was doing or moving forward, he'd simply shut the world out. Had stopped caring about anyone. Had withdrawn into his mind, into his books, into his career. Even when he'd met and married Jacqueline, he'd designed his marriage to fit around his life. And of course, it had fallen apart in a spectacular fashion.

Because somewhere in the past fifteen years, he'd stored away his heart outside himself. And then, suddenly, he didn't know how to forge a connection with his own child.

"I know a little about being in dark places, feeling like you'll never crawl out of them." The words flew out of his mouth. "Or feeling as if you deserve to be there."

"Don't tell me the great Nasir Hadeed hit points of low confidence in his esteemed life."

"I will save you from the gory details, then," he said, trying to inject humor back into his voice. "It is not a good feeling when our idols turn out to be hollow, no?"

"I didn't idolize you," she said with a fake outrage he didn't buy.

He worried that she'd probe. It was unfounded.

It was becoming more and more apparent that Yana wasn't anything like the flimsy illusion she weaved for the entire world.

"So, are you in agreement about me having Zara for a month?"

"If I insist on being present while you do?"

"Because you don't trust me to look after her?" she asked with big eyes. In that moment she looked as beguilingly naive and full of insecurities as his five-year-old. "I'd never put Zara at risk."

That it was a promise and not some outraged declaration made his chest ache. "No. I want Zara to see that we're not at each other's throats."

She nodded, taking his lies for the truth.

He had no intention of spending time with her on a regular basis, no intention of seeing her again after these three months were up.

And still, he wasn't able to help himself from prodding her. From poking at her sudden composure.

Suddenly, it felt as if he was standing behind a wall she'd erected. He shouldn't miss the messy, volatile Yana he'd once known, but he had a sudden feeling that this defensive barrier was a fundamental part of her.

"If that's a problem for you—"

"You keep thinking I'm still hung up on you. I'm not. Haven't been for a very long time. It might even be the right thing for all of us, because who knows how much time you actually give Zara. This way, you'll be forced to take time off from your work."

And there was the truth, putting him in his place in the perfect way. As only she could. "Yes, fine, you can spend time with Zara every year. But we don't have to put it in a contract."

"We do. I don't trust your good opinion of me will last forever."

And that was, apparently, that.

Pushing out her long legs, she reclined her seat and closed her eyes. Her arms were folded around her midriff, thrusting her small breasts up.

It took him seventeen long seconds to look away from the enticing picture she made even in repose, from her shiny hair to the deep cleavage at the V of her blouse to the long legs bared in pink shorts.

She was right.

He had no idea how the aftermath of these three months was going to look. Because the truth he'd refused to accept until now was that this woman had always threatened his control. Had always pushed and prodded at all the rules he'd lived his life by. She made him want to risk everything again all over. She made him forget the excruciating pain of loving and losing.

CHAPTER FIVE

"Yana? Wake up."

Yana tightened her arms around the solid warmth that enveloped her, needing to sleep for another thousand hours. "Get off. Leave me alone."

A soft tap on her cheek, followed by a chuckle, tickled the blurry edges of her consciousness. "We're here. Let's go, sleepyhead."

She was warm, and cozy and so tired, and the voice sounded so good against her temple. Like a deep bass reverberating through her, weaving a web of comfort she'd rarely known. "That's not how you wake up someone," she mumbled, snuggling closer and pouting.

A sigh and a hiss disrupted her pleasant state.

"Ahh... Would you like me to try the Sleeping Beauty method? I don't know my fairy tales properly but I think it involved a kiss."

A kiss? That deep, husky voice was offering a kiss to wake me up? Would it be as delicious as he sounded?

It wasn't a bad way to wake up, even though she'd always found the idea of someone kissing her to save her a bit problematic.

"Come on, Yana. Unless you want me to act on that threat."

Slowly, she blinked her eyes open and found amber-colored eyes gleaming back at her in the dark interior of the car. They were like warm, deep pools, inviting her to sink into them. She frowned. Something was wrong with the cozy picture, in and out of her head. In the past ten years, she'd only ever seen those eyes staring at her with contempt or anger.

It was Nasir. But why was Nasir offering to wake her up with a kiss? Was she dreaming again?

The car came to a sudden stop, forcing her to take stock of the surroundings. Through the tinted windows of the chauffeured car, she spotted a dark gray twilight sky, punctured by thick, tall trees that seemed to stand to attention, watching their arrival.

Her eyes widened as she realized she was in the car with Nasir and that they'd finally arrived at their destination. When he handed her a tissue, she stared at it blankly. A sigh left him before he gently wiped at the corners of her mouth.

Yana sprung back from him as if he were a viper flicking his forked tongue at her. Slowly, she pulled her limbs away from around him, even as her body bemoaned the loss of his solid warmth.

"It's okay. You're okay, Yana," he said so softly that the incongruence of it froze her. He'd never spoken to her with that tenderness. Not in ages. "You fell into an exhausted sleep," he added.

She wiped the corners of her mouth with the back of her hand and repeated the same to gritty-feeling eyes.

"Why am I not surprised that you are such an aggressive cuddler when you're asleep?" he said, a hint of humor peeking through his tone.

"It's information you shouldn't have at all," she quipped, feeling irrationally resentful. Though she knew he'd said it to put her at ease.

"No?"

"No. It's intimate information that's reserved for a lover or a boyfriend or a…"

With a groan, she closed her mouth. Why had he let her wrap herself around him like a clinging vine? Why not be cruel in action as with words and push her away? Then she wouldn't feel this discombobulated around him.

She straightened her shorts and her satin top, which was so badly wrinkled that it looked like she'd writhed on the ground.

No, just in his lap, a wicked voice she'd thought she'd left behind piped up.

With the guise of fixing her hair, Yana tugged

at the roots roughly, to restore a measure of sanity to herself. "Where's my jacket?"

One long finger carefully held her unwrinkled pink jacket aloft. "You kept saying you were too hot."

"You should've woken me up or pushed me aside."

"You really think me an unfeeling beast."

"Yes. And I'd like to keep thinking that."

"And why is that?" The soft query came with a silky, but nonetheless dangerous, undertone.

Yana took the jacket from him and pushed her arms through the sleeves, ignoring him. Gathering the messy mass of her hair, she quickly braided it away from her face. Only when she felt a semblance of composure return to her did she turn to face him. "I'm sorry for—" she moved her hand between them, her cheeks heating up "—climbing all over you."

He exhaled in a sibilant hiss, pressing his fingers to his temple. "It's no big deal."

"It *is* a big deal. You're my employer, and I'd like to keep those boundaries clear."

A flicker of irritation danced in his eyes. "Pity you didn't have that rule all those years ago, huh?"

And just like that, the truce that had lasted the whole flight fell apart. Grabbing his wrist, she pulled it up to thrust the platinum dial in his face.

"Wow, you lasted a whole nine hours without insulting me. That's got to be a record."

His long fingers grabbed hers. "Wait, that's not how I meant to say it."

"Let me go, Nasir."

"Not until you hear me out."

Of course she knew who he was talking about—Gregor Ilyavich, a sixty-six-year-old infamous painter of celebrated nudes. When he'd approached Diana, who'd also been her manager and coach back then, about painting Yana nude, her mother had been ecstatic. Just as she'd guessed, his nude portraits of Yana had instantly shot her into a new stratosphere of fame. All the big designers had wanted her face on their brand, were willing to pay whatever she wanted.

But the true price for her starry fame had come later—when Gregor had made his move on her. Something Yana chose to believe to this day that Diana hadn't known about. She herself had been a naive idiot who hadn't seen the power play until it was too late.

Thank God the portraits were now out of circulation as a private collector had bought them for millions. Not that Yana hadn't loved them. They had been gorgeous, otherworldly, elevating her to something more than the symmetry and perfection of her face and body. Gregor had pinpointed and then extrapolated things she'd chosen to hide from the world in those portraits—her insecurity and her vulnerability.

But the lurid gossip about her affair with Gregor, the over-the-top speculation that *she* had trapped him for his money, and her tattered reputation as some kind of backstabbing gold digger had left a bitter taste in her mouth.

Her justly deserved humiliation at Nasir's hands two years prior and then the flaming mess that had been her association with Gregor had been enough to confirm her belief that she was never going to get it right with men. Just like Diana.

"Are you forever going to dig up skeletons from my past and dangle them in my face? Is that the plan for the next three months?" A scornful laugh escaped her. "Because we both know there's enough material."

"No. Of course not. I brought it up the wrong way. I just…"

"Just what, Nasir?"

"I introduced you to Gregor at that release party for my novel. I felt responsible." A muscle jumped in his cheek. "I *feel* responsible, to this day."

Her righteous fury leeched out of her, leaving a void in its place. A void that would fill with dangerous things like hope if she wasn't careful. And even with that warning, she couldn't help but say, "What does that mean?"

"You were a very gullible twenty-one-year-old. He was notorious for charming and seducing women who were decades younger than him with the promise of fame and fortune. I was responsible for bringing you to his notice. For letting him enter your life. I hate that he...took advantage of you. That I didn't protect you."

"I was twenty-one. And Gregor coerced me in no way to pose for him. So there, I absolve you of all blame." She raised her palms, forestalling the distressing topic.

"Yes. But I should have looked out for you, should have made sure you knew his background. Abba took me to task for it enough times."

The mention of his dad was enough to make a lump rise in Yana's throat.

Izaz Hadeed had been one of the kindest men she'd ever known. Enough that she'd loved living in his home when Diana had been married to him. Enough that she'd known whatever had brought them together wouldn't last long because Diana didn't know what to do when good things came into her life and so she destroyed them.

Something Yana thought she'd inherited from her mother, in her lowest points, along with good skin and thick hair.

Enough to know that his son—while grumpy and caustic on the outside—had inherited that very same kindness. God, the stupid dreams she'd weaved, imagining them all together as one big, forever family.

Even after he and Diana had separated, even after Yana's own horrible shenanigans and false claims about Nasir kissing her, Izaz had always kept in touch with her. Calling her on her birthday, sending her gifts wherever she was in the world, asking her if she was okay after Nasir and Jacqueline's wedding…he'd made her feel like a cherished daughter.

He'd loved her like one.

She bit her lower lip with her teeth hard enough that the pain held back the tears that threatened to spill. "Ahh, so that's what this is about. Izaz Uncle finding fault with you. That's why it still rankles after all this time."

"It wasn't just Abba's criticism that got to me…" His chest rose with the deep breath he took. She knew it was raw grief at mentioning his father, who had passed not a year ago. Only Izaz's affair and subsequent marriage to Diana had been the biggest divide between father and son—conquered and forgiven years later when he'd reconciled with Nasir's mom. And yet, she remembered Izaz being heartbroken that Nasir hadn't forgiven him completely, that his son had become a hardened man in the subsequent years.

"It rankles, still, because it's true."

In a sudden move she didn't expect, he clasped her cheek with a gentleness that shocked her.

When she'd have pulled away, he held firm. Something about the expression in his eyes threatened to break her into so many pieces. His second hand joined the first one, in this assault of kindness.

She felt locked, pinned, splayed wide open.

"The world only saw your confidence, your success, your brazenness. But I know now, as I should've known then, that you were young, naive, so unused to the vipers and Gregors of the world. I should have warned you that he was a predator."

The genuine regret in his eyes forced out an answer. "He didn't...do anything I didn't want him to, Nasir. And if mistakes were made, I was twenty-one and so I'm allowed them."

She didn't know why she was propagating yet another lie between them when she could instead choose to clear the air and admit that she'd refused all Gregor's advances. Especially since it seemed Nasir's main regret, that he hadn't interfered, persisted after all these years.

"That mistake shouldn't have happened in the first place. You should've been—"

She slapped his hands away, his gentleness nothing but a hidden strike. "I think I prefer the version of you that blamed me for my impulsive, lazy, ruinous tendencies rather than this...patronizing one that invalidates my very existence. How dare you feel sorry for me? Or is it disgust over my actions and how you should have saved me from myself that keeps that massive ego of yours boosted?"

"Yana, you misunderstand me."

Without waiting for his clarification, she pushed the car door open and stepped out into the dark night.

She was so very exhausted—all the way down to the marrow of her soul. Just when she hoped that he saw her, *actually saw her*, and was beginning to respect her, he set her back to square one. And however many times she promised herself never again, it didn't seem to stick.

Her legs felt like they were made of that JELL-O that Zara adored as Yana stepped out of the car without falling face-first into the rough gravel. Not that she'd have managed even that without Nasir's steadying arm around her shoulders.

Once she could trust her legs, she quickly moved out of his reach. His scowl told her he hadn't missed her instinctual rejection.

She rubbed her eyes again, all the different time zones playing havoc with her body's rhythms. There was a chill in the air that nipped at her bare legs and chest. She inhaled deeply anyway, loving the scent of pine and something old in the air. Tugging the lapels of her jacket closer, she raised her head.

It was a big castle—no, strike that—a humongous castle that greeted her. Rather, it was the shadows and outlines of one, since twilight had now given way to thick, dark night. The castle looked like it had sprung right out of one of Nasir's stories. The stories that were situated perfectly at the periphery of dark woods, the ones that housed all kinds of scary and outcast creatures. The ones she'd always liked the best because she'd felt like she'd belonged in them.

Once he straightened, she reached to take her heavy shoulder bag from him. He held it away from her.

She ran a circle around his body, trying to reach for it, bumping into him. "It's fine. I can carry it inside."

"You're being ridiculous, you know that?" When she jumped for it, he circled a hand around her neck with a gentleness that made her pulse leap. The gesture was so unlike him, so much bordering on possessiveness, that she stilled. Every atom in her body stilled. "It's just a damned bag, Yana. Let it go."

Yana raised her hands in surrender, an unholy humor coursing through her at his cursing. There was nothing better than seeing him devolve to her level—whether in vocabulary or gestures or actions. Suddenly, power and something else between them felt more fluid than she'd ever assumed.

"Where are we?" she asked, following him as

he began an upward trek from a gigantic courtyard where the chauffeur had dropped them off.

Small, hidden lights dotted across the land illuminated a gravel pathway toward the looming castle. All the tension she'd felt while imagining them together melted away as she took in the fresh air and the beautifully dark setting.

God, she and Zara would have so much fun here. And yet, she didn't miss the fact that it was also quite the deserted location for a five-year-old. Zara would need other kids and activities to engage with. But she couldn't bring that up now. She'd love to never bring it up and not give him a chance to put her in her place but that wasn't an option.

Zara was, and would always be, a priority, even if that meant courting Nasir's special kind of disapproval. She made a mental note for later.

Apparently, they weren't going to walk in through the main entrance, which boasted two solid iron doors with knockers the size of her head. She felt like she was entering a fantasy world.

"It's a small village near Bavaria," he finally answered. "Close to the Alps. You'll see the view tomorrow."

The remoteness of the location was exactly how she'd imagined he lived. Had Jacqueline played queen of the castle?

Jacqueline had been quite the party animal,

and their relationship had never made sense to Yana. But she'd put it down to her own conflicted past with him.

Now she knew that she'd been right in her intuition.

The closer they got, the larger the castle loomed with dark gray stone, and tall turrets and, oh, my God, a tower at the back that seemed to look down on the rest of the castle. "There's a tower in your castle?"

"Yes." His laughter at her enthusiasm reverberated in that single word.

"Please tell me you're renting it or I don't know…housesitting it?"

It was all a little too close to one of her fantasies. Fantasies involving castles and Nasir and dark, fairy-tale-esque romance had been the staple of her teenage years. Fantasies she needed to keep convincing herself she'd grown out of.

It was as if all her darkest dreams were taking shape in reality—she and Nasir in a castle, she and Nasir with a lovely little girl, she and Nasir finally meeting under one roof as equals. But there was no danger of that, she reminded herself bitterly.

When Nasir didn't loathe her, apparently he was busy feeling sorry for her.

She sensed his reluctance before he answered her. "No. I bought it. Recently."

"How recently?"

"Right after Jacqueline died," he said, meeting her gaze. Letting her know that he knew what she was doing. "We moved here from her Paris apartment once I took care of the legalities."

She took a shot in the dark. "You bought it to impress Zara?"

The moonlight didn't hide his grimace. "She wouldn't stop talking about castles and fairy tales and dark creatures. You'd left us—" he raised his hand, forestalling her protest and shook his head. "You're right. I shouldn't rewrite history. *I* made you leave. Jacqueline was gone. All Zara would talk about was living in a huge castle with three monstrous dogs and with a forest in the back and…" A long sigh seemed to emerge from the very depths of him. "It was the only bridge I had to build toward her."

"Oh."

He nudged her shoulder with his. The playful gesture stunned her. As did his teasing tone when he said, "I know where she gets that fixation from."

"I just shared everything that fascinated me at her age," she whispered, her mind scattering in a thousand directions.

What had changed in how he saw her? Had he finally understood that she'd always had Zara's best interests at heart? Was that enough to redeem her multitude of sins? And what happened when they didn't agree on something regarding Zara? Would his approval vanish?

"Stories saved me when I was a little girl. *Your stories* helped me escape my own life."

"I'm glad, then, that I got something right with you. Even if it was done unknowingly." His gruff tone hit her low in her belly, the soft underside she sometimes forgot existed.

Something built in the silence between them as he opened the relatively small but actually giant side door, and ushered her toward a dark staircase. And it seemed to stretch and stretch and stretch upward. Endlessly.

Without rancor or contempt or anger or intense mutual dislike coloring and cluttering the space between them, they were unmoored suddenly. As if anything was possible in that space now. As if they were any other couple who were trying to do their best for a little girl they both adored.

"I… I wanted Zara to have the same anchor during a hard time in her own life," she said, clearing her suddenly thick throat. "I didn't mean to create an obsession you'd have to deal with."

"No. I'm grateful for the spark of the obsession you planted. It became a lifesaver for us both."

He rubbed a hand over his face, and suddenly, in the dark corridor, Yana saw his own exhaustion, the emotional toll the past few years must have taken on him. Jacqueline's infidelities, her long battle with cancer, then her death and the full responsibility of Zara's well-being. Then suddenly, he'd lost his beloved father.

It was a lot for one man to take.

Even someone like Nasir, who was fully in control of himself and his emotions and the people around him and even his own circumstances. He was judgmental, ruthless, exacting in his standards for himself and others. And yet, now, beneath all of that, she saw something else, too. Something like regret.

Even just within the past month, he'd followed her wherever she went around the globe, all the while giving time to his own work and returning to see Zara every weekend so that she didn't feel abandoned yet again. It annoyed her how her heart ached for a man she needed to hate.

"Nasir, I'm—"

"You were a better parent to Zara than Jacqueline or I have ever been. For that, you have my eternal gratitude."

Stunned beyond words, she stared at him. That arch of electricity, that taut tug of connection, came again. This time it built faster and louder and stronger.

She nodded and walked on up the stairs, his words sitting like rigid boulders on her chest. Of course, he'd recognized that she loved Zara. And being the man he was, he'd immediately thank her for it, would give her the place she wanted in Zara's life. It was more than she'd expected when she'd said yes to this…contract, the best outcome she could've hoped for.

Relief should have come. Or at least some kind of vindication. All she felt, however, was a confusion, an ache.

"I feel like Maria from *The Sound of Music*," she said, forcing a giggle into her tone. The last thing she wanted was to have an emotional breakdown in front of him, for him to see the wretched confusion in her soul. "Please tell me you don't have several children waiting for me to look after."

"That's a nice fantasy," he said, a thread of some deep, dark, cavernous thing dancing in his words.

Yana stumbled so hard that she almost fell on her face.

His fast reflexes meant his hand on her jacket held her upright just as they reached the landing on the second floor.

"What? Lording over me and Zara like Captain Von Trapp with his whistle? Finding fault with everything I do? Because let me tell you that particular fantasy's already come true."

He opened the door, a grin on his face. There was something really different about him, here in this place. Or was it simply relief that he finally had her where he needed her? "Why do you always assume that I want to think the worst of you?"

"My dear stepbrother," she said, using the term she knew he loathed, placing her palm on his chest in an exaggerated pout, pouring on her fake charm thick, to dissipate the fizzy bubbles in her own chest more than anything else, "it's our history that says that."

His long fingers wrapped around her wrist but he didn't drag her touch away. Her pulse raced under his fingertips, playing a symphony for his favor. "I don't remember it always being quite like that."

"Weren't you the one who taught me that history always has another version? Probably from the one who didn't originally have a voice?"

"What is your version, then, Yana?"

"Does it matter anymore?"

"It clearly does. To both of us."

She shook her head, telling herself it was a lie. "I made a ghastly, horrible mistake, no doubt about it. I knew I'd done something wrong the minute I told Diana you kissed me. I want you to know that I did eventually tell Izaz the truth. I was… I own my part in that, even though I'd like to say I was also a product of insecurity and codependency and…" She sighed and blew out a long breath. "You meted out a rather cruel punishment that would've lasted a lifetime if not for the fact that I came into Zara's life, quite by accident, which ended up, *luckily* for me, perhaps redeeming me a little bit in your eyes."

If she thought he'd dig into the very painful past and pick at the scabs of her *ghastly, horrible mistake*, Yana was proved wrong. If she thought he'd jump at the truth she'd just revealed that his punishment to cut her out of his life had hurt her, she was safe from that, too.

He simply stared at her for a long time, as if weighing her words. "You are right. And you're a better person than I am, clearly, for not holding it over my head."

A humorless snort escaped her. "That's what you expected when you came to see me, wasn't it? Me to hold your own behavior over your head? That's why you were so fast to use all the leverage you had on me."

"And you refused me, again and again, even though I know you want to be here for Zara. Don't think it escaped me that the possibility of being here with me was so distasteful to you that it sent you into a faint."

"Nasir—"

"Don't think I forget for one minute that my beastly behavior toward you might have cost Zara the stability she needs, the love of the one person she desperately craves. I might have failed my daughter all over again."

There was such a note of anguish in those words that Yana found herself reaching for him automatically. In that moment Yana remembered why she'd once admired him so much. There was a quiet dignity to him, even in defeat. "I didn't mean—"

"My relationship with my daughter is a mess I created. I let my unhappiness with Jacqueline, my distaste for her drama, create a divide between Zara and me. I assumed she was better off with her mother than being used as a pawn in a power play between us."

"A little girl would only see it as apathy," she said, unable to help herself.

His throat moved on a hard swallow and his mouth curved in a bitter smile. "I realized that too late. I got so good at keeping people out of my life that I succeeded with my daughter, too."

It was as natural as breathing to want to comfort him. "You and she will get through this, Nasir. I promise you. Things will be better soon."

With his hand at the small of her back guiding her through the darkness, and the tight corridor they were navigating, their gazes held. "You don't know that."

"You're doing everything you can to fix it. Including kidnapping me, blackmailing me, letting me drool all over your Armani jacket in my sleep. Just to make her happy. Just to give her a sense of security. She'll realize all the effort you're putting in soon enough. Zara's a very clever girl."

It was what she'd have done for anyone in such a situation. She'd always been a very touchy-feely person. But when her upper body pressed against

Nasir in a tight, warm squeeze, she realized too late that she'd gone too far.

Too far with him, that was.

Because even a little was always too far with this man.

Suddenly, it was impossible to ignore her nipples pebbling against the muscled wall of his side. Her breasts aching and heavy. His hard, denim-clad leg nestled between her thighs, against the place where she'd dreamed of him being so many times. Her spine and her curves melting and molding around him to get a better fit, a tighter squeeze, a harder push.

She closed her eyes, and it was a mistake because the sensations multiplied by a million. Her breath came in soft, shallow pants as she searched in the darkness with her fingers. A liquid ache pulsed through her when she found purchase on his face. His soft, warm mouth that could be so hard with anger at her fingertips. The rough, pebbled texture of his scar. His breath on the back of her hand, heating her up even more.

And without her permission, without her knowing, without her will involved, her body bowed toward him. Offering itself up as some kind of ritual sacrifice at the very altar of the beast she should run from.

Forehead pressed against his shoulder, she breathed in long gasps, willing herself to let go. To step back.

His fingers around the nape of her neck were like bands of heat, brands of possession. Lingering at that sensitive place. Playing through the little wisps of hair there.

"Yana," he said, his own voice a husky whisper, echoing around the walls. "We can't… I can't do this. There's too much at stake."

She jerked back from him so fast and with such force that the hard stone banged into her head, evoking a pained gasp. Hot tears pooled in her eyes at the impact but he was already there. His fingers gently probing and prodding at the back of her head.

She took a tentative step away, putting herself out of his reach. "I'm okay. Let's just—"

"Yana, we can't—"

"No idea what you're talking about," she said, focusing her gaze over his shoulder. "All I did was offer comfort. Maybe even that's not palatable to you when it comes from me."

He searched her gaze in the dim light and nodded. But the truth of their almost-encounter shimmered in the amber depths, and her own senses, whipped into a frenzy of need, taunted her for her lies.

CHAPTER SIX

"WAKE UP, YANA AUNTIE! Auntie, wake up!"

Yana found herself tickled by small hands, but this time she knew who was wrapped around her like a baby koala. Her eyes opened to shafts of pure golden sunlight sliding in through the high windows, bathing her face in a warm light. For a second she lay with her open gaze focused on the high, vaulted ceilings, and yet another gleaming chandelier that reminded her of the castle and her and Nasir's almost-encounter.

Nope, not thinking of the thing that he claimed he couldn't give in to and that had never even happened. Although, the fact that he'd said that he couldn't take the chance...meant he wanted to do it, whatever it was that hadn't happened, right?

"Yana Auntie!"

Smiling, Yana trailed her fingers to her stomach where itty-bitty fingers were digging into her ribs, and caught them with her own. "Gotcha, Zuzu!" As she expected, Zara gave a loud squeal and burst into giggles when Yana shouted,

"Tickle monster!" and went for the little belly. Like earthworms in mud—another favorite of Zara's—they rolled together on the bed, giggling for God knew how long.

Her chest burned as if a fire had cleansed away all the loss and grief, leaving fertile ground again. There was nothing like laughing and goofing around with Zara, who gave as good as she got. Eventually, they both ran out of breath.

Sitting up, she pulled Zara into her lap. Tiny arms immediately wound around her neck, with her face buried in Yana's chest. An almost claw-like hold of those little fingers raised a lump in her throat. Yana buried her face in Zara's thick curls. The little girl smelled of sunshine and dirt and strawberries, and it tugged at instincts Yana hadn't known she had.

She'd never given much thought to marriage or children, to stability and putting down roots. Planning her life was Mira's forte, and believing that it would turn out wonderfully was Nush's, whereas hers had been drifting from one mess to the other. And yet, ever since she'd been a chubby, charming baby, Zara had sunk her hooks into Yana's heart and they only seemed to dig in deeper with time.

"You pwomised you'd visit soon." The complaint came in a small, muffled voice as if Zara wasn't sure she had a right to even complain.

In response, Yana grabbed Zara's huge stuffed

toy, and spoke to Lila the llama. She told the stuffed toy about how both her grandparents had passed away in the past year, and how much Yana had needed to be around her sisters and why she'd not been able to visit Zara sooner.

Pulling back, Zara stared with a seriousness that belied her tender age. "Your thaata died?"

Yana nodded.

"Like Mama?"

Hand shaking, Yana tucked a springy curl behind the girl's ear and planted a soft kiss on her chubby cheek. "Yes. But—" she trailed her fingers over the little girl's face and neck, straightening her pajamas, slowly tickling her again, forcing an easy cheer into her voice "—I'm not sad anymore. Now that I can hold my Zuzu girl again."

Explanation accepted, Zara sneak-attacked her, and they burst into another bout of giggles, made plans for picnics and walks and movie nights and ice-cream parties. The number of promises the girl elicited from Yana restored her faith in her decision to come.

Suddenly, three huge, excited dogs burst into the bedroom and began to sniff and bark and generally make mayhem around the bed. "And who is this?" Yana asked, eyeing the two shepherds and the pug.

One castle and three dogs... He really had gone all the way in making Zara's fantasy come true. Yana shouldn't really be surprised after his ruthless determination to get her here. How much further would he go to make Zara happy?

"That's Leo and Scorpio. And that one," Zara said, pointing to the cutest among the three, "is Diablo."

As if he knew how extra adorable he was, Diablo the pug lifted his front paws up onto the edge of the bed. Yana patted the sheets and immediately, the three dogs jumped up and went for their faces, licking them.

Zara suddenly fell quiet.

"What's wrong?" Yana asked.

"We're in twouble." Resolve tightened the little girl's features. "Don't worry. I'll tell Papa I let them on his bed."

Belly dipping, Yana noted the austere navy-blue furnishings, the starkly functional furniture and an entire wall full of bookshelves that shrank the vast bedroom significantly. The bed was a vast king bed with two night stands—one full of Zara's pictures in frames and the other held a pile of books and a pair of reading glasses.

This was Nasir's bed. This was his bedroom. Yana sighed.

Why did all roads seem to lead her to Nasir's bed?

"I let the dogs on the bed, Papa. Not Yana Auntie."

Nasir stood still at the entrance to the room,

wondering if his heart could rip out of its shallow shell at the entreaty in his daughter's words. The doubts in her eyes tore him apart, reminding him yet again how badly he'd messed up with Zara.

"Don't send her away."

Hands on Zara's shoulders, Yana pulled his daughter into her body, as if she meant to protect her from everything, including him.

As if she were my own... He hadn't missed Yana's almost slip of the tongue that evening at the nightclub. The picture of them together like that on his bed—one achingly adorable with jet-black curls and the other, glowingly beautiful with dark golden waves spilling over her shoulders, packed an invisible punch to his sternum. With the sunlight limning their similar golden-brown coloring, they looked like they belonged together.

They looked right, real in a way he hadn't known in so long.

Shaking his head at the fantastical thought, Nasir moved toward the bed. With each step he took, Yana's mouth flattened.

Did she truly think him such a beast as to upset his own daughter over something so small? That although he'd unknowingly made Zara doubt his affection, it made him feel any less awful? Or like Zara, had he only shown Yana the grumpy, grouchy outer shell he'd adopted long ago?

Going to his knees, he gazed into his daughter's eyes. His hand shook as he straightened the collar of her pajamas. "It's true Papa doesn't like dogs in his bed. Because Papa's a grouchy old man who's used to things a certain way. But sweetheart, you'll never be in trouble with me over such a small thing. And definitely not your wonderful Yana Auntie, either." His five-year-old's lower lip jutted out in disbelief. "I pinkie promise that I'll never send her away again, yeah?" He extended his pinkie toward her and he wondered if his heart had moved into that digit now.

That trembling lower lip calmed and Zara tangled their pinkies. Her smile was a wide beam of sunshine. "Next time I'll close the door so they don't follow me."

He laughed and buried his face in her belly. "You're not promising that *you* won't sneak into your auntie's bed every morning, are you?"

She threw her arms around him again and with the sweet scent of her in his lungs, his pulse calmed. He bopped the tip of her nose before getting to his feet.

His gaze shifted to Yana, and in an instant, a full body flush claimed him as he took in her disheveled state. Her face free of makeup, her wild hair tangled around her shoulders, she looked incredibly young and vulnerable. As if she'd put away the mask she wore for the world. Something almost like approval glinted in her eyes.

"I'm sorry she woke you. I held her off for two hours."

"It's fine. Clearly," she said, waving her hand around the bright sunlight in one of those expansive gestures he was coming to recognize she made when she wanted to hide, "I overslept."

She asked him something in fragmented Arabic while trying to protect Lila the llama from the dogs so that Nasir had to move closer to hear her. When she repeated it, he laughed. Apparently, it was a morning of shocks. Or the month of Nasir pulling his head out of his backside. "You just asked me why you're standing in my bed."

Pink dusted her cheeks and she grabbed the duvet as if she needed a lifeline.

Seating himself next to her, he ignored how stiff she went. There was a wicked joy in making her brazen act falter. "When did you learn Arabic?"

Her sharp profile softened as a gentle smile wreathed her mouth. "When I lived with your dad. He practiced..." Her eyes shimmered with an aching fondness as she swallowed and corrected herself. "He used to practice with me all the time. He taught me a lot of bad words and said I needed to use them against you."

"He always liked you."

"He *loved* me." Her conviction shone so bright and clear that Nasir was taken aback. "He loved me as if I were his own daughter. He'd call me and text me and send me little gifts. Even though you forbade him to have any contact with me."

The profound ache in her tone made Nasir swallow hard. "You kept in touch?"

Her smile grew bittersweet. "Usually me venting about how the world was unfair and he'd remind me that the world didn't understand how wonderful I was." The love in her eyes made him feel like he was lost in a sea of emotions he'd willingly turned off inside him.

It *had* been his condition when his father had reconciled with his mother that he never have any more contact with Diana or her daughter. On an intellectual level, he knew why he'd insisted on that. Diana was destruction itself. And yet, he hadn't given a moment's thought to the fact that Yana had gotten caught in the crossfire. He hadn't wanted to punish her, even though she'd lied about him kissing her. He simply hadn't considered the effect on her of taking away his father's love.

"I did a lot of things wrong by you. I won't shame myself further by offering excuses."

"You thought I was beneath your notice. But he…"

"He what?"

She cast a quick look at Zara and the dogs, who were now playing on the terrace attached to the bedroom. "Izaz Uncle wondered if you never forgave him fully for leaving your mother. He thought the bond between you two never…

recovered fully." She held his gaze. "I believe he missed you. *The real you*, he'd say."

Standing up and moving away from the bed, Nasir rubbed shaking hands over his face. Regrets coated his throat like thorny prickles. "Of course I forgave him. My mother wasn't easy to love," he said on a wave of grief. "I... I wish he had just asked me. I'd have told him that it was all to do with me. Not him. He was a wonderful father whatever went on between him and Ammee." He turned to her, feeling caught between the sterile world he'd locked himself into and this new one where pain and loss ruled. "What else, Yana? What else did he say?"

"I'd console him by calling you all kinds of names." Her mouth twitched. "And he'd defend you, say you'd just lost your way. That his warm, loving son was buried somewhere beneath the cold, hard one you'd become."

And here was the proof—that the man who'd loved him with such depth, who'd believed in second chances, had thought Nasir had just lost his way. His father hadn't approved of his lifestyle, or his marriage to Jacqueline, but he'd never interfered because he'd believed that everyone had a right to make their own mistakes. Unlike his mother, though, Abba's concern had been about Nasir's happiness.

Nasir had not just lost his way, he'd actively distanced himself from all the good things in his life. Because losing Fatima had been so painful that he hadn't wanted to feel anything again.

A sympathetic murmur had him unclenching his jaw. He turned to find Yana looking at him with regrets in her eyes. That she could feel his pain when he'd been anything but kind to her… humbled him. "I didn't say it to hurt you."

"I know that."

They stared at each other, she from her cozy position on the bed, he standing under the archway leading to the terrace, as if at a crossroads.

She'd always been an incredible temptation. Easy to resist because she'd always embodied the very drama and loss of control he'd abhorred. And yet now, in revealing his own flaws to him, she was revealing herself to him. Bit by tantalizing bit. Anything between them could only be temporary, yet she was here for his kid and he shouldn't even indulge the mad idea in his head. But it was there, growing every second. He wasn't even sure if he could walk away from her again, like he'd done last night.

"I'm glad you and he kept in touch," he said, forcing his thoughts back. "That he could talk to you about…me."

She nodded. And he could see questions fluttering on her lips, her curiosity in the arch of her brows. He waited. And waited. And waited. The Yana he'd known once wouldn't have half the control she seemed to possess now. Even that felt like a loss to him.

Turning away to look at Zara, she said to him, "Why did you bring me to your bedroom?"

"I was as exhausted as you were." He thrust a hand through his hair as she slowly untangled herself from the mess Zara and the dogs had made of the sheets. A toned thigh, the flash of her pink thong and the shadow of her nipples— the artless show she gave him was sinfully arousing. He cleared his throat. "I think I automatically brought you here because it's the bedroom that's attached to Zara's."

Distaste filled her eyes as she jumped from the bed as if it might take a bite of that delectable bottom. "Wait, this is the room you shared with Jacqueline?"

"No, I told you last night, remember, that I bought this castle for Zara after Jacqueline died. You know as well as I do that she'd never have moved out of Paris for anyone or anything."

She kept moving until she was standing directly in front of shafts of sunlight. As if they couldn't resist her, either, light beams drenched her, delineating every rise and dip for his pleasure. Golden dust motes created a crown around her stunning face. Her legs…went on for miles, and it was only the background noise that Zara and the dogs created that stopped his thoughts from crossing over to forbidden territory.

"If you can have the staff show me to a new room—" Yana stepped back as he approached, a frown tying her feathery brows. "What?"

He grabbed a colorful throw from the foot of the bed and wrapped it around her, tugging her closer until the edges met in front of her chest. But he didn't let go. He didn't want to. There was something incredibly arousing about arresting her in his embrace, in having her face him like this. Gathering her messy hair, he pulled it back so that the throw could sit snugly around her shoulders. The brush of his knuckles over her nape, her rough exhale coasting his lips, every moment was pungent with an arching awareness.

Tying the edges of the soft throw to hold it together, he backed away.

Licking her lips, she stared at him.

"Your T-shirt is practically transparent."

Yana's belly did a slow, tantalizing roll. Her mouth dried up as if she'd spent hours in a desert. Which she had once for an underwear ad. But this was a delicious burn that seemed to taper off and arrow straight down to her pelvis. She tugged at the T-shirt she'd put on last night, far too exhausted to unpack properly. No bra and a thong with most of her legs bared.

In contrast to her disheveled state, Nasir was dressed in dark jeans and a white T-shirt that made his olive skin gleam. His wet hair was piled high on top, with gray streaking his temples.

But neither the casual clothes nor the gray in his hair or the fact that he looked like he hadn't gotten any sleep last night diminished the sexual appeal of the man one bit. It was too much. Her own skin felt too tight to contain the pleasure and anticipation sparking through her.

It wasn't just the magnetism of his good looks, though. This morning the strain around his mouth had lessened. He looked dreamy, carefree, even, approachable. And that it was because of her presence, even if only indirectly, made delight dance inside.

God, she was such a pushover, and the realization prodded her to brazen it out.

With one wriggle of her shoulders, she dislodged the throw he'd so gently wrapped around her, wishing she could shrug off the warmth of his body just as easily. Nakedness was nothing new to her. Her body, for so long, had been just a tool, another costume, that she put on to please the world. She wasn't going to feel shy or modest about it now.

She cocked a hip and straightened her shoulders in a move she could do in her sleep. "My transparent sleepwear is not my problem." The throw settled like a warm wrap around her cold feet. "Since you're the one who barged in here."

He grinned, and she had a sense of a passionate, almost violent, energy being contained in his body. "Right! The closed door means the dogs and I are forbidden to enter."

"You've got it wrong. Unlike you, the dogs *are* welcome. Even in my bed, Nasir," she retorted, incapable of keeping her mouth shut.

Palm pressed to his chest, he let out an exaggerated sigh that said it was his loss.

It was such a dramatic, outrageous gesture for him to make that she laughed out loud. A pang of nostalgia ran through her. He'd been like this once—playful, witty, as ready to mock himself as he'd mocked her.

And even this felt like madness, to laugh with him like this, to see him try so hard for Zara's sake, to see his eyes travel over *her* with that devouring intensity. The near chant in her head that he was just one of millions of men who derived pleasure at the symmetry of her face, at a body she'd achieved through hours and hours in the gym and nearly starving herself at the beginning of her career, didn't help one bit. It was impossible to see Nasir as just any man, even in her head.

"Anyway, I can't just take your room, Nasir—"

A new voice piped up, interrupting her. "No, she can't. It's bad enough that we have to see her making pretty eyes at you all over again. Didn't you learn a lesson with your wife, Nasir? Yana will only teach Zara more awful things about you."

Yana froze, recognizing that voice. Around her, a deafening silence fell. She felt Zara's little body tucking up against her bare leg and picked her up. Even the dogs seemed to know instinctively that they needed to be wary of Nasir's mother.

It took all she had to bite back a hysterical laugh because she didn't want to scare Zara. Already, she was stiff in Yana's arms. When she saw Ahmed fluttering behind Amina, Yana walked Zara over to him. "How about a picnic as soon as we get ready, Zuzu?"

Her head tucked into the crook of Yana's shoulder and neck, Zara gave her a doubting look. "Pwomise?"

"Yes, baby. It's a lovely day and we'll spend the entirety of it outside. Once you finish breakfast, grab your boots and your scrapbook, yeah? You live right in the middle of a forest. So we have to look for fairies, okay?"

"Fairies!" Zara beamed. "Don't be late, Yana Auntie," Zara said, leaning across into Ahmed's arms. No one could miss the worried frown wreathing her forehead when she cast a glance at her grandmother.

Another thought struck Yana and she rounded on Nasir as soon as Zara was out of earshot. "You've got Zara stuck here, miles away from civilization, with only *your mother* for company? She hated Jacqueline even more than she hates me, Nasir. Is it wise to expose Zara to her brand of cutting honesty?"

"I'd never hurt Zara by showing my dislike for her mother," Amina spoke up.

"And yet, here you are, pouring vitriol in my face the first morning I'm here." Yana's voice shook. "Are you so wrapped up in yourself that you can't see that Zara can sense your feelings?"

Refusing to give Amina another chance to attack her, Yana closed the massive doors to the bedroom right in her face and pressed her back to it. Now she knew what Nasir had meant when he'd said they'd have chaperones galore.

If it was possible that there was a person who hated her more than Nasir did, it was his mother. The woman who blamed Yana's mother, probably justly so, for destroying her marriage. The woman who loathed Yana for being *that woman's* daughter and the one who'd made up a fake kiss from her son.

To trap him just like her mother had trapped his father.

Yana grabbed her bag from the closet and turned to Nasir. "Please book a hotel suite for Zara and me."

"No."

"I'm not staying here with *her.*"

"Yana, listen to me."

"And you call me manipulative."

"I never called you that. Not even when you

lied about kissing me all those years ago. You're far too reckless and destructively honest to be manipulative."

"You're just saying those things to try and calm me down."

She walked through the vast closet, feeling betrayed. No one could spew vicious truths like Nasir's mom. And she was already defenseless, having barely recovered from her own mom's betrayal, and from the void her thaata had left with his death.

"You should've told me she'd be here."

"Then you wouldn't have come."

"Can you blame me?"

"Only Zara matters, Yana. Ammi knows that." He raised his palms in surrender when she glared at him, his jaw so tight that she could see a vein bulging there. "I promise, I won't let her near you."

"You *can't* ensure that, Nasir, unless you stick to me like last night's gum." A strange tsunami of emotions built inside her, and Yana couldn't grasp it back under control. That Amina might be right, that she'd lose herself all over again over Nasir...

"You can't control Amina...her grief, her loss, her...hatred. Not when they're all so raw after losing your dad just last year." She pushed her fingers through her hair roughly. "I get enough of this drama from my mom, and I've already had enough lashes about the past from you. I can't take it from her, too. Not even for Zara. Not when I'm trying to start a new chapter in my own life. Not when you both tried to make sure I lost your dad a long time ago."

Something about how still he stood arrested her frenzy. Yana knew she was losing it, betraying all the anger and resentment she'd tried hard to bury when Nasir had attempted to cut her out of his Dad's life, but she couldn't seem to stop. Not when he looked at her as if he was seeing her for the first time.

The real, messy, vulnerable, hurt-as-hell her. The girl no one had looked out for. The woman who'd thought she didn't deserve that kind of looking after. That kind of love.

"When I was growing up, I didn't know how deep words like that could wound. How toxic they could make me behave in turn. But not anymore. I can't keep getting battered by you and her, and my mom and all the shadows of my past mistakes. I'll fall apart and where will that leave Zara then?"

His fingers came around her nape in a firm, yet tender grip, stilling her. "Shh…breathe, *habibi*. Breathe for me, baby. You're okay."

"I—"

And then his arms were tugging her to him, and Yana sank into the embrace. It was a gift. As necessary as breathing. She'd been starved for touch for so long. Starved for understanding as she'd tried to hold her life from imploding. Starved for a lifetime of being held like this by him.

"You're safe here, *habibi*," he kept crooning at her temple, holding her as if she was the most fragile, most precious, thing in the world. Her breath came in shallow pants and she was trembling, and he kept whispering endearments as if he meant them. That bergamot and sandalwood scent dug deep into her roots, making a home there. Centering her. His large hands stroked all over her back, soothing her.

He'd been like this once before. A long time ago. He'd been kind and patient and... And he was only being so now because she was very near a breakdown and he needed her to not fall apart. He was a good father and would do whatever was required to keep her here for Zara.

She was in his life just because Nasir loved his daughter—she couldn't forget that.

"No lies," she said quietly, pulling away from him. "You decided it was okay for me to be exposed to your mother's vitriol. You're fine with treating me however you please because I'm an eternal car crash anyway, right? But no more. At least for Zara's sake, ask Amina to keep her mouth shut about Jacqueline." She wrapped her arms around herself, reminding herself that she was steel and ice. "I'll stay but you don't deserve it because you've broken my trust again."

After walking into the en-suite bathroom and closing the door behind her, she leaned against it. Yes, seeing Amina had thrown her. But she was stronger than an angry, bitter old woman, stronger this time than her childish attraction to Nasir. She'd be stronger for herself and for Zara.

CHAPTER SEVEN

NASIR STOPPED PRETENDING that he was getting any work done—even though it was a chapter he'd already plotted multiple times, minutes after he saw Yana walk to the pool with Zara's little hand tucked in hers. As he walked through the myriad corridors of the castle, their laughter floated upward from the multiple open terraces.

For over two weeks now, he'd told himself that work was more important, especially after the forced break while he followed Yana all over the world. But it was a fruitless exercise when all he wanted was to join them both and play happy family in a way Zara had never experienced with him and Jacqueline. Even that startling thought didn't stop his progress.

Every day, after walking the dogs, Yana and Zara promptly arrived at the pool. When Zara went down for a nap under the supervision of her actual nanny, Yana disappeared back inside the castle. Then the two of them would show up in the cozy library in the evenings, either reading or drawing or listening to rhymes. Yana even ate dinner with Zara. He didn't doubt one bit that Yana's day was precisely planned to have minimum intersection with his. Even during that early dinner, she retreated halfway through it to give him time with Zara.

It was exactly the kind of experience he'd wanted for Zara, with a few structured activities and free playtime, but had been unable to achieve with any of the myriad staff he'd hired. In only a couple of weeks of Yana's being here, Zara laughed, played naughty tricks and was more open and demanding with them—everything that a healthy, thriving five-year-old should be. Even his mother had to agree that Yana had an innate ability to love Zara like a mother.

With him, though, she was an ice queen extraordinaire. A thorn under his skin. The flicker of anguish when she'd said her pain was an acceptable price to him haunted him, day and night. The flash of grief when she'd said that she'd lost his dad, too, showed he'd become a villain in her life.

He knew he'd compounded his mistreatment of her by throwing her out after he'd learned that Yana was supposedly Jacqueline's character witness to enable her to gain solo custody of Zara. Having seen her open love for his daughter, he more than doubted his accusations now. Yana wouldn't have done that to Zara. Jacqueline must have instructed her lawyers to name Yana without telling her.

All of his distrust of her just because she'd claimed he'd kissed her when he'd never even touched her. It had been a stupid, juvenile impulse she'd given in to when she was only nineteen. Had he really behaved any better—a man twelve years older than she was? Had he shown any more maturity than she had?

Now she'd shut him out so thoroughly that Nasir felt as if he had been robbed of something he'd never even realized he had. He'd made peace with his attraction to her. But where did this need to be acknowledged by her come from? To be forgiven for all his multitude of sins?

Wherever it came from, it was so not a good idea. Especially when she'd always be a part of his little girl's life *and his life*. And still, he kept moving, instead of turning back.

Yana sat at the edge of the pool, praising Zara for everything she did right and for things she tried under the swimming instructor's tutelage. When Yana stood up, Nasir's breath left his body.

Her skin gleamed with a golden-brown sheen that came out of no bottle. The bright orange bikini she wore was basically three triangles that should come with a libido overload warning. Every movement sensuality in motion, she looked like a Bond girl from the eighties, all wild and free and innately sensual.

The swimming instructor and Yana struck up a relaxed conversation. Then she bent and lifted Zara out of the pool and wrapped her in one big towel, tying a turban-esque smaller one around her hair before the nanny came over to fetch the little girl for her nap.

"Do you see how she flirts with that boy? Is this the kind of behavior you want around Zara?"

Nasir's irritation leaped into dangerous territory at his mother's open insults. Of course, he saw the casual flirting, the laughter, the swat on the arm and how her body inevitably bowed toward the younger guy as she chatted to him, how she naturally made him open up and smile back at her.

What he hadn't understood until now was how that effervescence, that wildness, was an intrinsic part of her. Like lightning, she either illuminated or burned everything she touched. And just the idea of burning with her made arousal flood his body.

He cast his mother a quelling look. "Don't, Ammi."

"You will regret—"

"Stop, please."

In just a few minutes Yana had pinned down his mother's inconsolable grief and the outlet of bitter rage she used to channel it. The past year he had given in to his mother's demands to stay with Zara because he understood the sheer magnitude of her loss. He'd lost a woman he'd loved once. While Fatima's face was nothing but a distorted memory now, the hollow loss of it remained.

But now his mother's words were directly harming his own motherless child. That he hadn't seen Zara's reticence with her until Yana had pointed it out…made his very foundation flounder. "If you cannot be civil to Yana, I'll send you away."

"I'm Zara's grandmother. I've helped you look after her all these months."

"And for that," he said, "I'm forever grateful. I want Zara to know you, to love you. Jacqueline's parents are long gone anyway. But everything you say, everything you don't say, about her mother, and now about her precious Auntie Yana… Zara processes all this."

"She is only—"

"You can't have missed that any time Zara spends with you has to be overseen by me at her request, that it's out of obligation."

He could see her heart breaking at his harsh words but the truth had to be said. If she didn't fix her behavior, the damage would soon be irrevocable.

"You're choosing that woman who's a liar and cheater and…whose mother ruined my marriage over me?"

And there was the crux of the matter. "The only one I'm choosing here is Zara. I'm doing what I should've done from the moment Jacqueline told me she was expecting. If you can set your grief aside for one moment—" he raised his palms to hold her protest off "—you'll acknowledge that Zara flourishes when Yana is around. Yana's going to be a permanent part of our life, and I want you there, too. That means you have to let the past go. Yana was only a child herself when Abba and Diana met."

"What about the lies she told about you?"

"She was young and naive, and the only one she had to teach her right from wrong was Diana, who we both know has no moral compass. And I had just dealt her a brutal rejection." He'd never been able to get her stricken face out of his head. He'd turned on her, when he could have dealt the same rejection with a little grace and a lot more kindness.

Instead, mindless with grief and guilt over losing Fatima, he'd shredded Yana to bits. He saw the truth finally, clearly now. Yana had loved him with all the urgency and naiveté and fierceness of a nineteen-year-old.

"If I can let it go, then you can. And Yana's not responsible for Abba leaving you."

"You are attracted to her," his mother whispered in a shaken voice. "How just like a man!"

He didn't dignify that with a response.

"She is not right for you."

Nasir laughed. "I chose Jacqueline but she cheated on me again and again. And believe me, I was no great husband, so I very possibly drove her to it. Yana's suitability is moot because she loathes the very sight of me."

"That's impossible."

"No wonder my ego has always flourished, Ammi."

"If she's that important to Zara," she said, having to have the last word before she walked off, "then you'd better keep your distance."

Having been celibate for more than three years, Nasir wondered if part of what was driving him might just simply be sexual frustration. But he knew it wasn't just a need for release.

Yana's ice-queen act was rattling things he didn't want to delve into. It was time to take not quite a sledgehammer to it, because Yana was far more fragile than he had ever thought her, and not just in body. The most shocking thing, however, was this…strange energy between them. He understood now how much of her natural passionate nature went into hating him. And hating, he knew from his own experience from his marriage to Jacqueline, was not apathy.

He relaxed into the lounger while Yana took her own swim. Let the bright afternoon sun soak into his skin.

When was the last time he had taken a moment for himself like this? The last time he had found this pleasurable fizz run through all of him at the mere idea of a conversation with a woman?

In a smooth, single movement, Yana pulled herself out of the pool. Water glistened over golden-brown skin in shimmering drips, licking at toned muscles and lush valleys and hollowed dips that he wanted to chase with his own tongue.

Yana walked past him, as if he was no more than one of the statues littered around the estate.

Nasir wondered what his life might have been like if he hadn't dictated her life from afar, deciding rights and wrongs for her, and he'd never quite loathed himself more than he did then.

And like a statue brought to life by a sorceress's hand, he suddenly felt all these things he had shut off long ago, when Fatima, the woman he should've protected with his life, had died in his arms.

If she was disconcerted by the fact that he was waiting for her by the pool in the middle of the day when they hadn't even made eye contact for more than two weeks, Yana didn't show it by the flicker of an eyelid. Having toweled herself down briskly, she grabbed a tube of sunscreen and began to apply it to her belly and legs liberally.

Nasir saw all of this out of his periphery, and it

was as if she had stripped naked in front of him. Just for him.

The shimmery white gel soaked into her skin like magic dust, not that she needed it. Slightly angling her torso, she lifted her bikini top and took her breasts in her bare hands with a brisk efficiency that came from parading in front of strangers with a power only a few could own. Once the bikini top was back in place, she reached around her back, twisting herself like a gymnast.

He stood up and grabbed the tube of sunscreen. "Let me help."

She didn't even look up. *Ice queen indeed.* "I can manage, thank you."

He was damned if he walked away now. "Right, it makes you uncomfortable if I touch you. Forgive me."

The slender line of her shoulders stiffened. He'd have missed it if he wasn't entirely too fascinated by her body language. Tension drew a line down her back and spine, giving him a map to her emotions.

"And why would I be uncomfortable if you touched me casually?"

"I wondered that, too." He managed a shrug, somehow keeping his lips from twitching. "But it's a fair assumption based on how you keep jerking away from me."

She snorted and somehow even that was elegant, too. "My body is a tool. I've sold clothes, shoes, hairstyles, cosmetics, jeans and most of all, sex. I've had hundreds of photographers and designers and camera boys and tailors maul me about like I was a mannequin."

Nasir wished he could see her face, the bloom of pink on her cheeks, the little sparks that made her brown eyes glitter when she was aroused. Take her in as she was right now, instead of the icy wraith that had been walking through his castle recently.

But he forced himself to stand there, just a little behind her.

After exactly thirty seconds, she looked up at him. Determination written into every line of that achingly lovely face, she nodded at the plastic tube he was holding. He dropped to his knees by her thigh.

Awareness jolted into him at the aching beauty of her up close. Like an exquisite painting that bestowed some new boon every time he looked upon it.

Chin tilted up defiantly, she presented him with her back. He pushed up the messy tendrils from the nape of her neck, while tugging at the two fragile strings holding the bikini top there with the other. And then the one below.

Her forearms rose to hold the loose top in place, thrusting those perfect breasts into a cleavage that he could unwittingly see perfectly from his vantage point. He didn't know if he should feel like a voyeur or be glad that his libido was back with vengeance. Shuttling those thoughts aside, he poured the sunscreen liberally into his palms and began to rub it down her back.

Smooth golden skin and toned muscles under his palms—he shouldn't have felt such sensual, sensory pleasure in the simple action, and yet Nasir could feel himself getting harder by the second. The contact was innocent and nonsexual, and yet heat seem to arc between his fingers and her flesh, something he could tell she tried her best to hide, but failed.

"As long as I have your attention," she started, and Nasir smiled, because he knew she was trying to distract herself. Was it all simply want on his part and hate on hers? Or was there more?

"If I had known you were looking for my attention, I would've insisted that you stay on for dinner after Zara goes to bed."

She shivered under his hands. "I'm taking the evening off."

"When?"

"Tonight."

On an upward sweep of his hands, he found tight knots at her shoulders. "For what?"

"I need a night off."

"Has Zara worn you out?" When she stiffened, he quickly added, "Quite the prickly thing, aren't you? Anyone would be worn out and begging for adult company when one spends most of their waking hours endlessly running around after a five-year-old."

He pressed his fingertips gently into one stubborn knot and heard her soft moan. The sound went straight to his groin. Thank God she couldn't see him because at this point, he must look obscene.

"I have castle fever," she finally said.

Somehow, he infused humor into his words when all he felt was a tsunami of inappropriate wild urges. "I thought you loved castles."

"As a fanciful teenager, Nasir. Castles are all well and good, especially when you think a charming prince lives in them but—"

"I'm the devil. Is that it?"

"More like a beast." Her answer was immediate.

He grabbed the bottom ends of the bikini top by reaching around to the front and almost grazed the underside of her breasts. Breath shallowing, he tied the strings at the bottom, and then took hold of the ones at the top. His fingers lingered on her neck, as he tried to keep the damp tendrils of her hair from getting into the knot. Her shoulders trembled as he touched the jut of her clavicle, marveling at how much passion was contained in such a fragile body.

Shooting to her feet all of a sudden, Yana jerked back. And he saw it then—the pink flush that shimmered under all of that golden-brown skin. And not just her cheeks or neck, but dusting the tops of her breasts. Her throat moved in a hard swallow that rippled down her chest.

"I apologize for hurting you," he said, transfixed by the sight.

Gears turned in his head, mostly driven by the molten desire in his blood. Truth dawned and held him in thrall—she definitely wanted him.

"I'm not going to break apart because you caused a little pain."

"But I should not cause it in the first place," he said, coming back to himself.

Knowing one of the most beautiful women in the world wanted him was a trip all on its own. But it was also a sop to his masculine ego that had taken enough dents with a partner who'd cheated on him as if she was picking a different weekly flavor of her frou-frou coffees.

But knowing that someone like Yana—vulnerable and innocent and full of heart and fragile—wanted him…was a honey-coated thrust to his insides. "Yana, I should like to talk to you about what you said the other day."

Grabbing a sheer white robe, she tied it at her waist with a fierce tug.

He had the most insane urge to pull those ends with his hands until she fell into him and he could burn the edge out of them both in the best way he knew.

"It's not necessary. As I've proved to you over

the last two weeks or so, I'm very much capable of having a polite relationship with you, Nasir. Please, let's not dig back into the past and play the blame game again."

"Even if it's only so I can admit to you that I've been inexcusably wrong?" he slipped in.

For a second, just a second, it looked like she would give him a chance to talk. Something almost like longing flashed in her eyes.

But then she was shaking her head, and her messy bun fell apart, and long, wavy dark gold strands of hair framed her face. In that moment she looked very much like a beautiful, naive prize that had been grabbed up by the beast. He was beginning to hate that damned fairy tale.

"A friend of mine will be here to pick me up around five this evening. I've already prepped Zara so you don't have to worry. She knows I'll be back tomorrow morning by the time her Arabic lessons are done. If you'll just inform security to let him through the electronic gates—"

"No."

"What do you mean, *no*?"

"I mean my security won't let him in."

He turned around and started walking away. That was not the end of it, he knew. But he'd had enough of kidding himself that he didn't want to explore this thing between Yana and him. Enough of his own lies that somehow he'd keep away from her.

Right now he simply wanted her company. Her forgiveness. Her wild laughter. Her eyes on him.

She grabbed him by the shoulder and turned him and thrust her face close to his, all warm, golden skin and exploding temper. "Is old age affecting your brain cells? Because I wasn't asking for permission."

He laughed.

That lovely, lush lower lip fell open as she watched him, drinking him in. Warmth crested his cheeks at the open, artless way her eyes stared up at him, as if he was exactly the tall, cold drink she needed after a swim in the afternoon heat.

"Oh, believe me, every faculty, even those I thought were faulty or dead, are now functioning at peak capacity. Thanks to you, *habibi.*"

Her mouth opened, closed and then opened again. Curiosity danced across her face and he willed her to give in, to ask him what he meant. But he lost. "Are you saying no to my friend coming here to pick me up or are you saying no to my going out?" Tiny lines pinched at the corners of her eyes. "What gives you the right to say no to me for anything?"

"No to both. For one, I don't want some random friend of yours finding out where I live. And second—"

"Have Ahmed drop me at the nearest village, then."

"You never asked for a day off when we were

talking terms." There was no way he was going to let her go off and see some male *friend*. He didn't care to examine his motivations just then. Maybe never. Maybe there was a freedom in going all in into becoming this ruthless, arrogant, uncaring beast she thought him to be anyway. "If it's not in the contract, Yana, it's not happening."

She pushed at him with her hand on his chest, but he didn't budge. And he saw now how volatile and touchy she got when her temper was riled.

Raising his hands, he gave her a sweet smile that he knew would only push her closer toward the edge. He wanted to see the explosion, the thundering temper, the impulsive, self-destructive step she might take.

And then he wondered what it would be like to be in the path of all that destruction she wreaked, to let himself be devoured by the storm that was this woman.

She stomped her foot, much like Zara did when she didn't get to eat her dessert before dinner. "Oh, how I hate you sometimes!"

"I prefer hatred to what you've been serving me up this past fortnight or so."

She colored. "I'm keeping my end of the bargain. I spend most of my time with Zara. I love spending that time with her. It's only for an hour or so during her nap, and then again after she has her dinner and goes to bed that I leave her. So why are you—"

He stepped closer to her, determined to not let her run out without giving him an answer. "Where is it that you disappear to? And what do you do? Don't tell me the party girl, supermodel extraordinaire, retires to bed at only seven in the evening?"

"That's none of your business." She shut him down so hard that it only made Nasir more curious. "As you've just mentioned, I'm not used to being tied down to one place for too long. I need a night out on the town."

"Where do you want to go?"

Her response was the cutest twitch of her nose in distaste. Something in his chest melted and he wondered how much of him had been frozen over the years to be constantly melting at each taunt and expression that she threw at him. And what would eventually happen to him if he didn't stop her?

"A nightclub. I want to go dancing… I have all this energy I want to get rid of." There was something so sensuous and yet, unpracticed in that little wiggle of hers that all Nasir wanted to do was see her do it again. And do it because she wanted his eyes on him. Do it because she wanted to please him.

"Give me a few days and I'll take you."

She laughed and it was like watching a sunrise captured in one of those time-lag videos. It was beautiful, and breathtaking and made his breath falter in his throat.

"You at a nightclub?"

"You sound more scared than excited at the prospect. What are you so afraid might happen?"

She swallowed and didn't meet his eyes. "If you come, it will become a big thing. I don't want to be photographed with you again."

"I thought you didn't care about being photographed with me. Your sisters know where you are, right?"

"It's not my sisters that I'm hiding from."

"Nobody can get to you here. I promise you that. You don't have to be scared, *habibi*." The endearment fell from his lips as easily as if he'd said it a thousand times.

"It's not what you think," she said. "It's just... I don't want Diana to know where I am."

He wanted to probe the source of the argument between them. Not that he was surprised at her wanting to hide. Diana had never been a good parental figure. For now he let Yana be.

Soon, though, he would have all her secrets. He'd lay her bare, see through to the real Yana she hid under the party-girl persona. Maybe that was the way to break this fascination with every facet of her. Maybe then he could go back to viewing her from afar with a mild interest at best.

"Have dinner with me in a few days. We'll

have guests over, since you're scared of being alone with me."

"I… Who?" Suspicion marked that single word.

"A few good friends of mine. You'll have good conversation and dancing choices other than me."

Her eyes widened. "Really? You're going to let your friends see me here at your forbidden castle? Has hell frozen over?"

"You're the one making all the assumptions here, Yana. And you won't give me a chance to dispel any of them. One might wonder why you need to retain them. Almost like armor, one could say."

He left her standing there, with her mouth open, incredibly frustrated with her and even more so with himself. But he'd brought temptation into his life, into his house, into his very bed even, and he had nothing left in him to resist her.

CHAPTER EIGHT

Yana was searching through her wardrobe for something to wear to Nasir's dinner party when she heard a knock on her door.

For a second she wondered if it was one of the staff to tell her that Nasir had rescinded the invitation. Because nearly a week later, she still couldn't process his change of heart.

Tolerating her for Zara's sake was one thing. Actively seeking her company was another. Although, she didn't doubt that he thought he was being all protective and honorable by keeping her out of trouble. Whatever his motive, though, she was far too tempted by this chance at a glimpse into his life to refuse.

She opened the door to find an army of people. Surprise made her gasp as Ahmed and a younger woman rolled in a dress stand, followed by Zara, her hand tucked into her grandmother's bigger one.

Yana followed Ahmed and the colorful display of dresses on the stand. "What's going on?"

"Nasir Sir thought you might need help with getting ready for tonight."

"Did he?" Yana asked, somehow keeping her bitterness to herself. "Does he think I'd embarrass his highbrow friends, Ahmed?" she hissed in a whisper so the others couldn't hear.

He shook his head. "This is my daughter, Huma," Ahmed said, beckoning the younger woman closer. "If it's okay with you, she wishes to dress you for the party."

"I was just going to wear something from my wardrobe," Yana added, wary of Nasir's new behavior. But the crestfallen expression on the younger woman's face made her feel horrible. "Of course, I didn't pack for one of Nasir's fabulous dinner parties. I'd love a chance to try one of your creations." She ran her fingers over a couple of evening gowns made of frothy chiffon and cut in simple, classic lines. Nearly a decade and a half in the industry had given her a discerning eye when it came to fashion. "These are gorgeous. Did you design these yourself, Huma?"

Pride and joy shone in Huma's eyes. "Yes, I'm studying fashion."

Ahmed gave his daughter a nudge. "Nasir Sir has already paid for her education. But she refuses to leave because she thinks her old papa cannot take care of himself."

Yana's heart warmed at the obvious affection between these two. Suddenly, she could see why

Nasir might have suggested to them that Yana needed help. It wasn't a big surprise that he was a wonderful human being when it came to other people. It was only her he held in such low esteem.

Even if it's only so I can admit to you that I've been inexcusably wrong...?

His question had been haunting her. Did he truly want to apologize to her? To begin a different sort of relationship? Could she bear that? Or was she letting him mess with her head again?

"I'd love to wear one of your creations, Huma, as long as you let me pay you for it."

Huma shook her head. "Not at all. It's a dream come true to see you wear one of my designs. If you'd just let me take a picture once you're wearing it," she rushed on. "I wouldn't share it with anybody. Not on social media. I just... I want proof that the gorgeous, stunning Yana Reddy wore one of my designs."

Yana squeezed her hand. "Of course you can share it. Between you and me, I'm kind of getting tired of the modeling world, but I still have my foot in the door there. I know a lot of photographers and design houses. I'll get you in touch with people I trust," she added, noting Ahmed's expression.

"I'm not worried about the kind of people you will introduce her to, Ms. Reddy. If they're anything like you, my daughter is in good hands."

Yana had no idea what she'd ever done in her life to deserve such genuine affection from him but she let it drape around her like a childhood blanket. "Now…" She clapped her hands, picked Zara up and settled her on her hip. "Let's see. Zuzu baby, do you want to help me pick a dress for tonight?"

Like an octopus, Zara wound her hands and legs all around Yana, as if she never wanted to let her go. For all the hours they spent together, Yana was still dreading the goodbye that would eventually come at the end of three months. As much as she hadn't wanted to be here, under the same roof as Nasir, she'd found that she liked living at the castle.

Especially since, whatever her son had said to her, Amina had kept her distance from Yana, too.

"To turn you into a pwincess?" Zara asked.

Yana laughed. "Maybe. Although I'd like to be a princess who saves herself."

Zara nodded, as if she understood the intricacies of adulthood and wanting to be someone who saved themselves. "But I'd love Huma's help with a dress and yours with my hair so that I can be a perfect princess. Even the brave princess needs all the love she can get."

"Yay, did you hear, Gwandma? Yana Auntie said I can do her hair."

Dragged into the conversation by her granddaughter, Amina offered a tentative smile. "Are you sure you want Zara's fingers on that lovely hair of yours? She's going to mess it all up."

"Oh, I don't really care, Amina. It's not like I'm going to walk the ramp tonight and face a thousand cameras." And yet, even the wildest, longest, hardest events of her career hadn't caused this…constant flutter of butterflies.

Was she a fool to look forward to the party this much? Where were all the promises she'd made to herself that she'd treat Nasir as just another employer?

"You will look beautiful whatever Zara does to your hair," Amina added, always wanting to have the last word, just like her son. "You're leaving modeling, then?"

Struggling to keep her shock off her face— the older woman had the hearing of a bat—she said, "Give or take a decade, Amina. It's not like I know how to do anything else."

The words left a bitter taste in her mouth.

She had to stop with the negative talk. And yet, the fact that she'd not been successful yet in placing her children's novel with an agent had left her in knots.

She wanted it so bad—this new, fluttery dream to be an author, to fill some child's life with escape and adventure and love, as Nasir's stories had done for her. But…she was terrified that she'd never make it. Never get it right. Never have what it took.

She could share the manuscript with Nasir and get his feedback and advice. And yet, the thought of him finding her talentless, or worse, laughing in her face, made bile rise up into her throat.

With Zara still on her hip, Yana moved to the huge vanity table that had been moved into the bedroom the second day of her arrival. It was the most beautiful thing she'd ever seen, and she had seen a lot of beautiful things in her life. With three different panels of mirrors, it was truly a princess's possession. She had no doubt Nasir had acquired it in some rare auction, but she wondered every time she sat in front of it why he'd had it installed in here when she was still using his bedroom. "First, I'm going to do my makeup, okay? Something soft and..."

"No, Yana Auntie. Glittery... Pwincesses have glittery makeup."

Everybody laughed and Yana groaned. "Oh, pumpkin, you don't want your papa's guests to make fun of Yana Auntie, do you?" she said, unable to keep the biggest fear that had been haunting her ever since Nasir had issued the invitation, out of her voice. More dictate than invitation, though, she thought wryly.

Whatever she heard in Yana's voice, Amina came to stand behind her. "First rule of being a woman—never let men decide if you're good enough for them."

She gave the older woman a quick nod in

the mirror and wondered if she'd imagined the glint of satisfaction in her gaze. "Well, let's get started," Yana said, truly excited now at the prospect of getting ready for the night ahead. "With this many fairy godmothers, I'm sure I'll look beautiful tonight."

Yana entered the dining room and came to an awed stillness.

An otherworldly quality permeated the room with its grand sweeping ceilings and archways leading off to yet more rooms, like it belonged in an old film with its brightly lit sconces, gleaming chandeliers and the black-and-white-checkered marble floor. Through a huge archway, the room segued into an open, airy ballroom, where a couple was already slow dancing. With jazz playing on a record player and a low hum of conversation, it looked like one of those intellectual soirees she'd never felt good enough for.

The hum died as every gaze turned to her.

A huge stone fireplace blazed on one side in contrast to the French doors opening into a wide terrace with a view of the mountains. Cigar smoke drifted in from the terrace through the doors and lingered, adding to the dark, mysterious atmosphere of the room. Along with smoke, cold fluttered in, making one side of her deliciously chilly versus the warmth on the other from the fireplace. It was as magical as she'd imagined.

First impressions bombarding her, she noticed that it was an intimate group of guests. That meant less chance of losing herself. Her nervousness grew, thrashing it out with the excitement she'd been feeling all day.

It felt like an audition she was entering to find herself worthy of Nasir's highbrow group. And even if she didn't fit in, so what?

Bolstered by those thoughts, she straightened her shoulders. Her gaze moved over four couples, finally landing on Nasir, standing next to the huge hearth. His gaze swept over her, gleaming brighter than the amber liquid in the decanters on the bar cart.

The bright pink chiffon cocktail dress she and Huma had agreed on showed off her tan perfectly. It dipped low in the front with a beaded corset hugging her breasts tight, leaving her back bare all the way almost to the upper swells of her buttocks. It wasn't the most daring dress she'd ever worn and yet, maybe it was the most daring for this company.

It was cleverly held together by two straps tied at her neck, and that had reminded her of Nasir's fingers on her nape as he'd reknotted her bikini strings, and the delicious sensations that had engulfed her.

She didn't know how long they stood like that,

gazing at each other across the room, quiet murmurs all around them while the jazz crooned to a soft, sinuous beat, and the sounds of the night drifted in from outside. All of it felt like an inspired, perfectly orchestrated soundtrack for this moment.

"So this is why you've been avoiding us, Nasir. You've got this beautiful creature hidden away in your castle." A deep voice quipped from her side, breaking the pulse of tension between her and Nasir. For a fanciful moment, she wondered what kind of vision she'd need to see it arc between them like a rainbow, fizzing with electricity, tugging them closer.

A second voice chimed in. "Our Mr. Hadeed is not as conservative as he'd have us believe."

Yana turned to face the two men, their arms around each other, both stunningly good-looking in completely different ways. She nodded, her mouth curving into a smile at the easy camaraderie they offered.

Nasir was moving closer. Only years of faking a snooty haughtiness helped her swallow the awed gasp that rose to her lips.

Dressed in a casual black jacket, white shirt and black trousers, he looked like one of those larger than life heroes of the silver screen. Hair slicked back, that long beak of his nose standing out, a cigar dangling from his fingers, there was a magnetic quality to him that made her greedy for every detail.

Yana let herself look to her heart's content, let herself feel the sensation of desire drench her, let her senses fill with the sheer sexual appeal of the man. She could live for a hundred years, and she knew she'd never find a man more attractive to her than he was.

Reaching her, he tucked one braid that kept falling out of its clip behind her ear. "Your hair-style is…enchanting."

Yana laughed, trying to cover up the heat she felt at his casual touch. "Only a dad can come up with such compliments for his five-year-old's handiwork."

His brows rose. "You let Zara do your hair?" She nodded.

"Ouch. She gives me head massages and I know how painful those can be. Somehow, I managed to talk her down to once a month." He watched her with that intense scrutiny. "I finally told her that her poor little papa will lose all his hair if she continued in that vein."

Instantly, her gaze moved to his thick, wavy hair. The gray at his temples had only added to the appeal of the blasted man. Her fingers itched to sink in and tug and stroke, until he was putty in her hands. "I see no risk of that."

"You look…delicious enough to eat." He took her hand in his. A casual touch but his fingers were rough against her soft ones, and Yana felt the contact deep in her core. "No, not just eat. Devour."

She stumbled, a helpless longing slithering through her, as if he was a sneaky snake charmer determined to wrest out all her secrets. His palm at the small of her bare back was a warm, steady weight.

He hesitated, just for a second, and then took a look at her bare back. Yana smiled. She knew she looked good most days in most outfits. Her beauty had long ago lost any personal meaning to her, if there ever had been any. It had become a tool—even a weapon to wield if Diana had had her way, a means to earn a livelihood, something to oil and feed and care for so that it ran smoothly. For a long time she'd even felt a strange dispassionate apathy toward it because she'd thought it had led her to make bad decisions, starting with this very man.

But hating oneself—one's body, one's mind, one's weaknesses—she'd learned was one of those toxic traits that hollowed one out. She'd always thought her little sister Nush was the most perfect, achingly loveliest, woman and yet Nush, she knew, thought she looked odd and weird, just because she didn't conform to some arbitrary beauty standard.

So Yana had learned to at least respect her body, her looks, her face, even if what she showed the world wasn't exactly what she felt inside. But tonight... Tonight sheer pleasure fluttered and tightened low in her belly when Nasir looked at her. She reveled in the soft grunt of his exhale, in the stunned expression that had come over his face when she'd walked in, in the way his long fingers danced tantalizingly over her bare back.

Already, she felt drunk on pleasure.

"That dress should come with a warning label." There it was again—a husky timbre to his voice that he made no effort to hide.

"It was our unanimous choice for tonight. Huma's and mine."

"No wonder she was so eager to dress you. You look sublime in it."

"All these compliments... You make me wonder what the price is going to be." Instantly, she wished she could take back the words. She wanted to enjoy tonight, didn't want to dilute it with acrimony and accusations about the past. And yet, she was the one who'd gone there.

"There is a price," he said with the smoothness that made her feel like a gauche idiot. Her temper had always gotten the better of her. And she'd never been more aware of the fact than when she was with him, enveloped in his cool control and stoic rationale. "I wish for you to simply enjoy the evening."

Shocked, she darted a look at him. Found him staring back at her. Swallowing, she nodded. Something in her responded to his offer of truce. "I'll try. Believe it or not, the last couple of years haven't left me a lot of time or energy for living in the moment, or any kind of enjoyment, for that matter."

She wanted to smack her forehead with the heel of her hand. Apparently, she couldn't do artificial banter. Either she went too far with her anger or too deep with her confidences.

His fingers tightened over hers. "Come, let me introduce you to this rowdy crowd. Stick to me, and you'll be safe."

When he patted her on the back of her hand, it made her giggle.

His gaze dipped to her mouth, an eager frenzy to it, as if he wanted to taste her smile. "What is so funny?"

"You? Rowdy crowd?" She taunted him, even as she wondered exactly how he would introduce her.

A new swarm of butterflies took flight in her tummy. Who would he say she was? Zara's extra nanny? His ex-wife's BFF? His problematic, once-upon-a-time stepsister he couldn't wait to be rid of? His employee? Or a woman forever in his debt?

Her nerves jangled as he nudged her toward the grand table in the center of the vast room. As if he had beckoned them, his friends moved up from their various lounging positions across the room.

He didn't let go of her hand or loosen his grip around her waist. If she wasn't so nervous at the prospect of meeting his intimate friends, she'd have called his hold of her possessive.

"This is Yana, a close family friend. She's doing me an enormous favor by helping Zara settle down here after the last year."

A close family friend...

She liked the sound of that less than she should. Actually, she loathed it for how...sensible and correct it sounded. How it hovered in the space between them—a label, a barrier, the drawing of a line that shouldn't be crossed. And every inch of her rebelled at that boundary and she wondered if she'd ever be cured of this madness. Of wanting to be more to a man who'd never really seen her as a woman.

CHAPTER NINE

YANA FELT NASIR'S appraising gaze on her, as if it were a finger on her cheek. Somehow, she managed to keep her smile locked tightly in place.

His guests spoke at once, their greetings effusive enough to move the moment along. She shook their hands and couldn't help gushing when one of them was Nasir's longest standing friend and editor.

"Close family friend is so droll, Nasir. Especially the way you've been eyeing her from the moment she walked in," he said.

Before Yana could tuck his comment into a corner never to be opened again, one of the women spoke up. "This is the stepsister you're quite protective about?"

A chorus of reactions ensued, taking the whole secret stepsister idea and running with it. If it wasn't for the fact that she was tied up in knots about which one of her shenanigans Nasir had shared with the woman, she would've enjoyed the flights of fancy.

As if sensing her distress, Nasir's fingers tightened on the bare skin at her back.

The woman, sensing the current of tension pinging back and forth between her and Nasir, said in a whisper, "Nasir just wanted to know about what kind of emergency measures one might need to take with type-one diabetes. As the castle is quite cut off from immediate medical centers."

Yana couldn't help but send a glance at Nasir, perplexed yet again by his motives.

"I have made similar inquiries about Ammi's heart condition, Ahmed's ulcers and one of the staff's recurring back pain," Nasir said calmly.

She relaxed immediately.

Another gorgeous man, dressed to the nines, grabbed her by the waist with the charming insouciance she knew well from working in the fashion industry.

"Yana Reddy!" He kissed the back of her hand with a regal flourish that made her laugh. "Now I know why Nasir demanded that I come to this party. Usually, it's my partner James that he can't do without," he mock-whispered. "He knows the rest of this crowd is too boring and fuddy-duddy for a glorious creature like you."

Yana turned to the man who wouldn't bore her if they lived together for a hundred years. "Is that true?"

Nasir raised his palms in surrender, his gaze

holding hers in a silent siege. "Before you misunderstand my intentions yet again, I simply wanted you to have fun tonight."

Before she could respond, a short, squat man approached them. Recognition flared even as James introduced his famous musician partner.

"Where have we seen her before?" asked Dimitri.

"Other than the fact that she's a hot supermodel?" James quipped and then clapped. "Ilyavich's paintings. Her nudes were the best he ever did."

Comprehension dawned on Dimitri's face. But instead of the usual mockery or disdain, excitement lit his eyes. "That's it! You know, I've tried so hard to get my hands on one of those paintings. After that first private buyer got hold of them at the initial auction, they never surfaced again."

"I'm glad they didn't," Yana said. "I don't regret doing them, but the whole episode was ruined for me thanks to the dirty accusations I had to face afterward."

"It's almost like the buyer was looking out for you," said James, casting a pointed look at Nasir.

Yana's response misted away when she caught Nasir's reaction. Her skin pebbled into goose bumps. He knew who had those paintings? How? The next thought came like a torrent after the first. Strike that—he didn't just know where the paintings were.

He *had* the paintings.

Then she was being dragged away by a smug-looking James. But she couldn't help casting a look behind her.

Sure enough, the answer to her dilemma danced in Nasir's eyes. And Yana suddenly knew that she was in a lot more danger than she'd ever realized.

It was past midnight, and most of his friends had drifted off to various bedrooms when Nasir stubbed out the one cigar he'd allowed himself for tonight and sought the woman who filled him with adolescent anticipation.

His mother's warning about how necessary Yana was for Zara buzzed like background noise in his head, but made no difference as he walked toward her. Slow jazz was still drifting up from the record player and Yana was sandwiched between James and Dimitri, the three of them swaying to the soft beat.

"My turn," he said, taking her hand in his, and spinning her away from his friends. Despite her surprise, she came like a feather, light on her feet. Her delicious scent sank its tendrils into him, filling his chest.

She stiffened for a second before settling her hands on his shoulders. He wrapped his arms loosely around her waist, the bare skin there an irresistible temptation.

All evening it had been impossible to look away from her. But he also felt a kind of savage satisfaction in seeing the real, tempestuous, funny woman come out of that ice cocoon she'd spent the past few weeks wrapped in. She'd engaged in a rigorous discussion with his editor about books, given James and Dimitri a run for their money when they suddenly decided to start singing old melodies, and had generally been a warm, wonderful, passionate hostess, even if she didn't know she'd played the role so naturally.

Not even a month in, and already Nasir didn't remember what the castle was like without her. Without her and Zara's giggles and running around and playing hide-and-seek and making the staff join in and just generally filling the empty spaces in his life. But he was only an audience, as he'd wished to be for so long, instead of a participant.

Even the space and time between him and Zara was filled with how wonderful Yana Auntie was. It was as if she was a witch who'd cast a spell on all of them—even his mother. Proving every day what Zara and he had been missing, even before Jacqueline had died.

And now she was in his arms, a perfect, soft landing at the end of a lovely day.

They danced for he didn't know how long, simply letting their bodies move to the slow beat of the music. It was a sweet exhilaration even as tension buzzed and fizzed every time her thigh brushed his or his fingers found another patch of warm, bare flesh. His heart thundered as her hands drifted from his shoulders to his neck, then back again to his chest.

When she pressed her cheek against his heart as Ella Fitzgerald crooned, Nasir felt a sweet, poignant pleasure like he hadn't known in forever. The night was perfection, one he'd needed for so long. But what had made it even sweeter was that this woman in his arms was a mysterious, interesting puzzle that he couldn't stop wanting to unravel.

Sudden laughter from behind them made them both look at Dimitri and James, who were now singing at the tops of their lungs while clutching each other.

A soft sound fell from Yana's mouth and she looked down. To hide her expression from him, he was sure.

"What?" he asked, wanting to know every thought that crossed her mind, every emotion that made her sigh. His fascination was fast turning into an obsession.

"Nothing."

"Remember our truce?"

She seemed to come to some sort of resolution because her mouth narrowed into a straight line. Bracing for either his criticism or his mockery, he realized. "They are so...gloriously in love, aren't they? It's enough to make one..."

"Nauseous?" he asked, threading humor into his tone when he felt anything except laughing.

She slapped his arm playfully. "Why am I not surprised you find two lovers nauseous?" Her gaze dipped to his mouth, and then away. "I think it's magical. I've seen that kind of love between my grandparents. I think Thaata died so soon after her, because he couldn't bear to live in this world without her. They'd been through so much—my dad's alcoholism, bringing up three granddaughters... But their faith in each other sustained them. I see that in James and Dimitri. They're so lucky to have found each other and—"

"You think it's luck that they found each other?" he asked, genuinely curious.

"A stroke of luck, that initial meet-cute, where their eyes met across a raucous crowd, knowing James..." She laughed. "But I'm sure they work at it every day. I used to think it was magical when people just came together and stayed together. Now I know better."

"I don't think I'm interested in the formula, but I do want to know how you have learned that."

"I've seen my sisters. They're wonderful, accomplished, bright women. Caio and Aristos clearly adore them. But it hasn't been a cakewalk for either of them. There have been tears and drama and grief and pain..."

"You talk about them as if they're more deserving of love than you."

She shrugged and he thought his once petrified heart might crack open at the expression on her face. He pulled her closer, anger and tenderness twin flames in his chest. "You know that's not how it works, right?"

"I thought you weren't interested in love."

"I'm not. But it doesn't mean I don't understand it." Fury against everyone who'd wronged her, who'd led her to believe such utter nonsense, including himself, colored his words. "There's no metric you use to measure someone's worthiness. You should get that into your pretty head."

"You're lucky I find you sexy when you're all growly and bossy."

The husky half-mutter, half-whisper dropped into the space between them, sounding like what it was. A defense mechanism, a distraction. Not that it didn't get him all hot under the collar, egging him on to act.

"Are they okay now?" he said, curious to know how she fit in between them. How she talked of them betrayed how she saw herself, and he wanted to know more. And the more he learned, the more he realized how one-dimensional he'd made her in his head. For his own purposes.

"The difficulties they faced only proved that their relationships were worth working on, I think. Worth fighting for."

"You want this…grand, glorious love, then?" A faint tremor laced his words even as he told himself her answer wouldn't make a difference to their relationship. It wasn't anything he had to offer her.

"Yes," she said, blinking. "Although it took me a while to figure it out."

"You're not out there looking for this love?"

"As you know, dearest stepbrother," she said, her breezy smile not hiding the ache, "I'm trying to fix me first. No one wants a mess in progress."

"There's nothing to fix, Yana," he said, tucking another stray braid behind her ear. A strange sort of helplessness speared him that she should think herself less than any other woman or man. "Messy and imperfect and tempestuous and volatile and stubborn is all its own kind of perfection. I'm the intellectual fool who didn't see that."

The bodice of her dress shimmered as her chest rose and fell, tension shimmering like a dark cloud around her. "*Enough*, Nasir." Her eyes flashed at him, her cheekbones jutting out. "I've let you seduce me with words and compliments all evening. But the farce ends now."

"James?" Nasir called out, knowing that the storm was about to break. He wanted no witness to their sparring or her temper. He wanted no one else to see her like this—unraveled and glorious. His oldest friends waved goodbye and stumbled out of the room. The thud of the double doors was a loud gong in the bitter silence.

"I'm going to bed, too."

"No, you're not. Not until we have this out."

A flicker of fear flashed through her eyes before she notched her chin up in that characteristic belligerence that only aroused his baser instincts. "I'm not having anything out with you."

"I assumed a lot of things about you, Yana. Most of them in error, to my own detriment. But I'd never thought you a coward."

That stopped her, as he knew it would.

"How dare you? I've never in my life backed away from anything."

"Then why are you so intent on running from me?"

"Because I'm tired of dancing to your demands. Because I don't trust you."

And because I still don't trust myself with you.

Yana swallowed that last bit, though.

The whole evening, Nasir dancing with her, talking with her, laughing with her, arguing with her about important topics, asking her opinion—all of it had possessed a dreamy, surreal quality. His friends welcoming her as if she was a part of them, as if they were privy to the secret but well-known knowledge that there was a *them* that was made up of Nasir and her, had gone straight to her head and heart. As if she'd inhaled a hallucinogen that provided her with a real-life version of her deepest hopes and secret fantasies.

She should've never agreed to the evening. Never dressed up for it. Never enjoyed his gaze on her. Never agreed to the truce and flirted with him all evening. Because now she was standing in a quagmire that only pulled her in deeper and deeper.

She'd never been able to resist Nasir—even when he'd misunderstood her, castigated her, loathed her—for some right and some wrong reasons. Now he had an agenda to win her over, which seemed to require her surrender, and she was definitely not ready for that.

Not again, not when this temporary fascination ended and she'd once again stand alone with her shattered heart in her hands.

"What's there to not trust?" he asked in a low, grumbly voice, and she knew that it was his truly annoyed voice. The angrier he got, the lower his tone, as if he was turning himself into a statue, determined to keep it all inside.

"Why can't you leave this alone? Leave me alone?" she said, and one of the braids done by Zara lashed against her cheek yet again. Having had enough of the charade, she gathered her hair and tied it into a messy knot on top of her head.

"I wish for things to change between us."

If he'd lobbed a grenade into her face, she'd have been less shocked. Breath didn't come to her lungs, much less words to her lips. Her entire body felt like it was seizing up on her, seizing on sensations and images she shouldn't be feeling or thinking.

She stepped back, away from him.

It didn't matter because he took a step forward, too, and Yana thought he truly looked like a beast then as he stalked her across the vast room, with the glittering sconces casting dark shadows on his saturnine features, iron-hard resolve etching itself around that luscious mouth.

"There's been too many years of misunderstandings and dislike that we've both nurtured with a lot of care. It doesn't wash off easily and I don't even want it to," she protested.

"No, you'd like to paint me as your villain for the rest of our lives."

"I don't have a different role for you. The die was cast long ago." Her words came out as shaky as she felt. "It's enough to be polite acquaintances, considering we have a child we adore in common."

He raised his palms. All evening he'd been reeling her in with his compliments and kind words but it was a false surrender on his part. Or a fake one. "What exactly is your complaint, Yana?"

"Why do you have those nude paintings of me?"

"I told you I felt responsible that I didn't warn

you about Ilyavich. But when I saw them—when I saw how gloriously he'd captured all the different facets of you, that urge to protect you from all the other, greedy eyes only became stronger. Even without knowing then that this persona you carefully cultivate is all a mask, I felt an overwhelming compulsion to protect your true self."

If he'd had the words scripted to cause maximum damage to her heart, he couldn't have done it better. His reasons were why she'd felt such relief that the paintings had never surfaced again. Still, she tried to fight the spell he was weaving over her. "Why go to such lengths just so that I had a good time tonight? Why are you being so nice to me?"

If she thought he'd laugh at her irrational questions, she had him wrong once again. His frown graduated to a scowl. "That's what's sending you into a tailspin? The fact that I'm finally treating you as you've always deserved to be treated?"

"That's not an answer, Nasir."

"Fine. I want you to feel comfortable in my home. With my friends. With me. I want you to think of my home as one of your main bases in Europe."

Her heart thrashed itself in its cage. "Why?"

"Because I want you to be happy." An exasperated breath rattled out of him.

Yana knew he could be infuriatingly stubborn—a dog with a bone, really, when he got stuck on something—it was one of the qualities they shared, but she'd never expected to be at the receiving end of that resolve.

It scared her that she'd caught his passing fancy, or his sense of fairness. And where it would leave her when he'd had enough. "When you visit us, at least," he added as an afterthought.

She was shaking her head, excitement and something headier washing away the dread and fear and insecurities and the little rationality she possessed. "Don't do this. Don't trap me. Don't—"

And then he was reaching for her, and his hands clutched her arms and there was such sheer urgency, such reckless, naked desire in his eyes, that she was the one rendered a statue now. "You're the most confounding woman I've ever met. How is it trapping you if I want to do the right thing by you?"

"Because it's all pity and for God's sake, Nasir, I don't want your pity," she said, sidestepping the minefield she'd created herself.

How did she explain to him that her stupid heart had never been able to distinguish pity from liking when it came to him? That she'd take the little interest he showed her, turn it into hope and hang herself with it?

"It's not pity if I want the best for you or if I want to share your burden or if I want to tell you that I'll be here for you when you come out of rehab for your gambling addiction. I want to be the friend I should've been to you years ago."

Yana saw the trap then and it was of her own making.

Lies and half-truths and misunderstandings… she'd built them so tall and high that he didn't even see the real her. He saw the illusion she'd created, felt sorry for the mess she'd showed him, because he'd decided with that arrogant self-righteousness that he'd had a hand in it, too.

The illusion not only didn't serve her anymore but also threatened to make her worst nightmare come true. "I lied to you, Nasir. Those were not my debts. I'm not addicted to gambling and I never was."

He blinked and she braced herself for his disbelief and doubts. But he recovered fast with, "Then whose debts were they?"

"Isn't my word enough?"

"Of course it's enough. But now that we're dispensing with the smoke and mirrors, I want the whole truth. How were you in such a financial hole, then?"

"It was Diana." The words were wrenched out of her from some deep cavern, and yet immediately freed her of their dark weight. Until this moment when she'd made it real, she hadn't realized how much the secret had gouged her soul. How the pain it brought had stayed inside her, pulsing and throbbing, hollowing her out.

He sighed. "Diana took advantage of you, again."

"Yes. She…cleared out my bank accounts last year. I took measures then. But she still managed to get hold of my credit cards, and she…maxed them out. All our assets are jointly owned since I started modeling before I was legally an adult. I'd thought I could trust her, but she forged my signature and sold the apartment in New York and the house in California. Even the few rare pieces of jewelry I owned…she completely cleaned me out."

"While you were busy looking after Jacqueline," Nasir said, finally connecting the dots. Seeing a picture emerge in which he'd been so eager to find fault with her when there was none.

"I don't regret it one bit," Yana said, memories softening her mouth. "I know she wasn't perfect, but Jacqueline showed me more love and acceptance and concern than Diana ever did."

"Your loyalty is laudable, *habibi*. Is that why you covered up her affairs?" He wasn't angry but his bitterness was clear. "You had a just reason to hate me anyway."

"That's unfair. I didn't let our past color my actions, Nasir. Even when you treated me as if…" She tugged at the neckline of her dress in a nervous gesture he was beginning to recognize. "Jacqueline was desperate to save your relationship."

"And yet, she kept cheating on me."

"You've no idea what it is to be in love, do you? And to be found wanting?" she said, vibrating with emotion.

"Love was never supposed to be a part of our relationship. She knew that."

"Don't tell me the great observer of humanity's foibles and flaws thinks relationships can work based on a chart and a few conditions?" Even now, sympathy and affection filled her words. "Jacqueline made mistakes. It doesn't mean she ever stopped loving you. She begged me to help her, to…"

"You must have known it was a sinking ship, Yana. She abandoned Zara to you to care for."

"By that time, she was drinking a lot, her modeling dropped off and her business took a dive and…then came her diagnosis. She became bitter, different from the warm woman I'd come to adore."

"You still looked after her."

"Is it friendship if we only show up for the good times?"

Hesitation flickered in her eyes before she took a deep breath. Steely resolve hiding a fragile heart—he was beginning to understand her now. And himself clearly, too, in her words. He had had all these rules and plans and conditions for his marriage and not a single one had served them well. Not with Jacqueline and definitely not with his own daughter. There was no way to shut himself out of the world without making his daughter think he didn't love her, either. Without the risk of losing her.

And here was this woman he'd thought he'd pushed to the margins, gloriously in the center of it all, lashing him with truth after truth. Instead of gentling his pain, all the rules he'd lived his life by had only alienated him from Zara and his father.

"And since we're on the topic," she said, straightening her shoulders, "I had no idea she was considering filing for solo custody of Zara. You spent little enough time with Zara back then. But she talked so much about you whenever she returned from the trips you took her on, and she sounded so happy that I knew whatever your complaints about Jacqueline, you were trying your best to be a good father."

Her words were a vindication to Nasir's ears.

Or maybe even a benediction and approval that he hadn't even known he needed. From the moment he had learned that Jacqueline had been planning to take solo custody of his daughter, using his alleged indifference to his own child, he had wondered if there was any truth to it.

He'd never planned to be a father, something Jacqueline had been fully on board with when they'd met. And he'd done his best to keep their marriage together even as they'd grown apart by the time she'd conceived.

So many sleepless nights, and he'd even wondered if he'd done such a good job of turning himself into stone that he felt less than he should for his own child. He'd wondered if Zara would be better off with her mother.

"I think Jacqueline never told me what she was planning because she must have known that I'd never agree to it," Yana added.

Nasir forced himself to meet her eyes. "I should have known that, too. My entire world felt upside down when I realized how I'd made my own child doubt my love for her. I was so angry and scared that I'd lose Zara that I lashed out at you. Not that it's an excuse."

He ran a hand through his hair, marveling at how wise she was even as she thought herself messy. But that was the magic of Yana, he was realizing.

She lived her life fully, loved so thoroughly that it was like watching a thunderstorm. Both spectacular and dangerous at the same time. And Nasir remembered when he'd lived life like that once, when he'd loved freely, lived dangerously close to the edge. And suddenly, he wanted to be there again.

There were two things he had to do. The first came easily enough.

"I'm sorry, Yana. On so many levels. For all the sins I heaped at your feet, when they were all mine. For being a beast to you."

But the second—to let her go when he knew what she wanted out of life was something he could never offer her—felt impossible to even contemplate. For the first time since Fatima died, he felt an overwhelming need to lose himself to his selfish desires. To drown himself in pleasure. To live dangerously just once more, even if that meant Yana would burn him through.

CHAPTER TEN

YANA DIPPED HER HEAD, unwilling to let him see her confusion and the little flicker of fear. Nor did she feel any vindication or relief from his apology. It was disconcerting to discover that his compliments had more than their fair share of an effect on her, though. Disconcerting to discover that all of her defenses were falling away, like the castle Zara had made out of rainbow-colored sand.

No, he was attacking her defenses, laying siege and shredding the lies and half-truths she'd surrounded herself with. To what end, though? Did he simply want to clear the air between them now that she was going to be a permanent part of Zara's life? Or was there more?

"What other secrets and half-truths are you using as ammunition against me, then?"

"Demands and more demands," she said, deploying her silken protest even as she was quivering inside. "And here I thought you were not the usual predictably powerful man who wants what he wants when he wants it."

"You've no idea what I want, Yana."

His angry tone was like a shot of adrenaline. When he treated her as his equal, when he took her on as she was, there was no bigger high. She tilted her chin, letting him see her fighting spirit. "You have not earned the right to my secrets, Nasir. Nor to my dreams or fantasies."

"And yet, if I cover this last foot between us and touch you, I'd bet I'd find you far too willing and ready to voice at least one fantasy, *habibi*."

She watched him, every word acting like a leaping pulse within her body. Every step of his creating an ache between her thighs. "And why would you want to do that?"

"Because I have this insane urge to corner you and catch you and strip you bare until I know all of you. You're a maddening puzzle I want to unlock."

"This is about your ego, then? Because I managed to trick you—"

"You and I both know this isn't to do with my ego or pity or friendship or Zara or the past. It's about you and me." Another step and she could see the scar that bisected his upper lip and raked its finger upward toward his cheek. And she saw the naked desire in his eyes and the steely resolve of his mouth, and every cell within her reverberated.

"So will you dare let me test my theory?"

He was close now, so close that she could breathe in the heady scent of his aftershave—another weapon in an arsenal full of them. Her breath was a shallow whistle in her ears.

She should've burned, or melted, or ignited with him this close to her after all these years, and yet, the moment seemed to spring out of her deepest, wildest dreams, and suddenly, she didn't know how to be, how to act, in this reality. Did she run or did she stay and see this through? Did she dare steal this moment and live it with all she had, or did she bind herself and back away from a lifetime's temptation?

Something hard dug into the small of her back, and she pressed herself into it even more, hoping the sharp pain would be an anchor tying her to the ground when all she felt like was flying away. And then he was within touching distance, and she stared helplessly like the naive, inexperienced virgin that she was.

All the roles she'd played in her life at being a brazen seductress who lured men to make bad decisions and led them to their doom hadn't taught her any tricks or tools to get through this. She hadn't let any man get this close to her at all, because she hadn't wanted any man like she wanted Nasir.

If he'd grabbed her and kissed her to prove his point—as so many men had done before, thinking her volatile temper and confident words meant that she would welcome their crude attempts at seduction, if he'd touched her and smiled that infuriating, winning smirk of his as if this was nothing but a game they'd been playing for years, if he'd taunted her with one more word—Yana would have been able to resist him. Could have told herself that after all these years, after all the pining and longing that had become an intrinsic part of her, she was better than he was; she was better than this moment.

His palms on the dark wood on either side of her head, he leaned closer and pinned her like a splayed butterfly with his gaze. And said the one thing that was her Achilles' heel, that shattered all of her defenses.

"I see you, Yana, the real you." His breath feathered the side of her cheek in a warm caress, his amber eyes gleaming with a feral glitter. "Finally, I see all of you. And the things I want to do to you..." A self-deprecating sigh fell from his lips. "We've come full circle, no?"

So long, for so many years, with so many people in her life, she'd longed to be seen, to be accepted, even as she'd hidden the greedy, needy parts of her away. All her struggles, all her pain, all her victories, all her defeats—had they led her to this moment with this man? Was life worth living, worth beginning at all, if she backed off now?

She braced herself as if one could brace oneself for drowning in a tsunami. Leaning closer, she pressed her mouth to the corner of his. "Test your theory, then." Then she took that lush lower lip of his between her teeth and bit down and said, "This, however, isn't surrender."

Tingles of shock and tendrils of sensation swooped when he returned her favor with a matching nip of his white teeth over her own lower lip. "Ah, *habibi*, I've finally learned my lesson. I'll never underestimate you again."

He smiled then and it was a roguish, hungry smile and it built into something more possessive and molten as his hands started moving over her willing flesh and she swallowed all of that, too, along with the heat and hunger of his lips, because he was kissing her and kissing her and kissing her. As if he, too, had been waiting for this moment for a lifetime.

She was spinning stories yet again but even her lies tasted sweeter when he kissed her like that. He tasted of cigars and chocolate and like the darkest decadence she could ever imagine. They went at each other like horny teenagers— nipping and licking and sucking and fighting for dominance, and it was exactly like she thought it would be. But also somehow better.

There was magic in the very air between them and she let it seep into every pore. His jacket was discarded, necklines were tugged aside for better access, for more. His mouth seemed to stamp his possession all over—her lips, her temple, her pulse, her neck, the spot below her ear, and still, he wasn't done kissing her.

She groaned as he sucked at her pulse, arrows of sensation skittering straight down to her pelvis.

"Who knew such a prickly thing could taste so sweet?" he groaned.

She grabbed the lapels of his collar and pulled in opposite directions until buttons were flying and she could palm the taut planes of his chest and then slide down to explore the ridges of his muscled abdomen. He was warm and hard, with a silky coating of hair that she loved running her fingers through already. She kept petting and stroking every inch of flesh she discovered as he buried his mouth at the crook of her neck and shoulder.

Within seconds he already seemed to know where to hit her the hardest. When he dragged his teeth against the pulse fluttering already at her neck, she groaned and wrapped her leg around his hip.

They stopped then, tuned in to each other on a level that terrified her. He was so deliciously hard against her, and she instinctively rocked herself into him, the need for completion a much more primal drive than fear or sensibility.

Somehow, he'd shuffled them across the marble floor, the cold tiles on her now bare feet a welcome relief against the heat pouring through her. She wasn't laughing anymore as her back hit the plush padding of the chaise longue that was tucked against the far wall.

Nasir was on his knees on either side of her hips, gazing down at her.

It was a new angle to find herself in, a new angle from which to look at him. Except for the sizzling sparks from the fireplace and the fast, erratic whistling of their own breaths, everything was dark and still and silent.

Reaching her hand up, she clasped his cheek, rubbing the pad of her thumb over that scar. Allowing herself one, *only one*, moment of tenderness. She wasn't sure if she would get another chance like this. And she wasn't sure if she would survive another one anyway.

His nostrils flared when she dragged her thumb to the center of his lower lip and pressed. His teeth dug into the pad before he closed his lips over it and sucked, and she felt the strong pull of his lips somewhere else.

She arched her body, chasing the pleasure, and he granted it. Heavy and warm, the heel of his palm rested against the sweet center of her entire being. She writhed under that warm weight, begging him with her hips to make it more. His fingers snuck under the fabric of her dress, caressing the silky skin of her thighs, and then they were pushing away her thong and tracing the outer lips of her sex.

Sensations and need forked through her, winding her tighter and tighter. Finally, finally, his clever fingers found her most sensitive place, and slowly, softly, rubbed the bundle of nerves up and down.

Her language became gasps and groans and filthy expletives as she chased the tantalizing caress of his all-knowing fingers. "What else do you need, sweetheart? Ask me. Tell me."

His gaze pinned her in place, a dark need glittering there, when her body itself seemed to be spinning away from her. She rubbed a hand over her breasts, the tight corset covering them adding to her torment and pleasure in turns. "Touch me here, please."

Bending low, he plucked at the beaded corset and when it didn't budge, he cut it open with that damned knife he kept on himself all the time. Her entire torso arched up like a bridge rising out of stormy waters as he rubbed one taut nipple between his fingers. "Every inch of you is perfection," he said, almost to himself.

Then his mouth was at her breast and he was doing some swirly thing with his tongue. His teeth were there, too, and his thumb kept drawing those mindless circles around her nub, and suddenly, she was right there at the edge of the world.

And when she fell, splintering into so many different parts, he held her and kissed her and soothed her and he put her back together again. Yana thought she might already be addicted to those strong, knowing hands, those wicked, wanton fingers and those sweet, taunting lips. And she wondered if she might ever do this with another man, even though she already knew the answer.

But right then, tremors of aftershock still quaking through her in soft ripples, with his scent lodged deep in every pore, with his arms enveloping her in a perfect cradle as if she was precious and fragile, she didn't care. She couldn't care about the future or that she didn't have one with him.

"Come, *habibi*. Let me walk you to your bedroom."

Those long lashes fluttered as she looked around herself like a baby fawn. As if she didn't know where she was. And still, in that state of near comatose bliss, her body leaned into him, gifting him with a trust Nasir didn't deserve but was selfish enough to revel in anyway. Just watching her climax with that reckless abandon was more sensuous than any carnal act.

After several long beats, she rubbed the back of her hand over her mouth and looked up at him. For a split second, he saw a strange kind of longing for him that he'd once seen in another woman. A woman he'd failed to protect despite her absolute trust in him.

Drowning in the madness that Yana effortlessly weaved over him, it was quite possible he was imagining things he had no right to imagine, much less should, if he had any sense. He'd never meant for his dare to get this far, either.

His body was strumming with unsatisfied desire, Yana was looking at him as if he was the answer to every dark desire she'd ever had, and he simply gave in to the sheer sensuous luxury of the moment.

"You're good," she said with a smile that stretched her lips.

He was struck by a tenderness he hadn't felt in so long, that he'd thought parts of himself had petrified out in that war zone years ago.

"I'm glad you think so," he said, tugging the sides of her sliced open dress together, but she slapped his hands away.

"The last thing I want to do right now," she said with a sudden sharp clarity to her words, "is walk through the castle like this, let everyone see you've dismissed me yet again and advertise my walk of shame."

Irritation he should have mastered colored his tone as he brusquely said, "We're two consenting adults. There is no shame here, Yana."

Her feathery brows came together in a bow. "I thought the same thing a long time ago."

"Yana—"

"If there's no shame in this, then why are you so intent on walking me back to my room?"

She was such a mix of calculation and vulnerability, a complex puzzle he'd never stop delighting in. But, he had to remind himself, she wasn't his to delight in. Come tomorrow morning, in the clarity of daylight, she might even regret this moment of madness and freeze him out.

Wasn't that the best idea, though, seeing as they could have nothing more than this one night? There was no future for them; he should make that clear to her, as he had no intention of committing to a third woman and having it go wrong again as it inevitably would. And yet, he had no taste for fracturing the satiated smile on her lips just yet. Or was he thinking with his ego again, imagining she wanted some kind of future with him? What if all Yana wanted was to get this madness out of their systems? Would one night be enough for her? With all their misunderstandings—mostly on his part—cleared up now, and with her place in Zara's life permanent, couldn't they just be two consenting adults with sizzling chemistry? Or was that him thinking with his painfully hard erection again?

"You have to know—"

She leaned up and claimed his mouth with a

possessive hunger that decimated the little honor he had left that he was trying to keep. On and on, the kiss went, with her nipping at him, licking him, then running away and having him give chase.

"Why do we have to leave when we aren't finished yet?" Leaning back against the chaise, she giggled. Contrary to that light laughter, her gaze swept over him leisurely, full of desire and need and unabashed lust. She scraped a long nail over his Adam's apple, and down his chest, running down each scar on his chest as if it were a map to some long-lost treasure.

"Unless it's because you're an old man and can only 'do it—'" she used quotes as if anybody could misunderstand her right then "—missionary style on the bed?"

He arrested her fingers when they fluttered near the zip of his trousers. "You're mad," he said, bringing her hand to his mouth and placing a kiss at the center of her palm.

She shrugged it off. That thread of irritation flickered again as it dawned on him why she did that. She didn't want tenderness from him. Only sexual touch was welcomed—an arrangement that should've suited him just fine given where his thoughts had been moments ago. And yet, that thorn was under his skin again. Although he was getting used to that, too, that painful, stringent awareness, like new skin on an old wound.

Like he'd never be sure of his own desires and thoughts when it came to her.

"I feel drunk. That's the first time I—"

He stilled.

She peered at him from under her lashes, something calculating flashing across that stunning gaze.

He cupped her cheek, a sudden urgency driving him. "What?"

She leaned into his touch as if his fingers weren't circling her neck with a possessiveness he could not control. "The first time I felt that kind of pleasure with a partner. Usually, I need my—" that cute little frown appeared between her brows again "—tools."

Awkwardness dawned at that strange word, and she shrugged. Something wasn't adding up. Under his continued scrutiny, color stole into her cheeks, dusting them a pretty pink.

"I meant my battery-operated devices." She rolled her eyes, as if he was being thick on purpose.

And then in a move that was clearly supposed to distract him, which it did successfully, she dragged a finger over the outside of his trousers, tracing the shape of his shaft. His erection leaped under her touch. When he went to arrest her fingers, she kissed his chin.

Eyes wide and soulful and full of longing studied him. "Now who's intent on shutting this down? Or are we still only dancing to your demands?" She pouted, to hide the very real emotion in her words. "Have you solved the puzzle that you labeled me? Is your fascination with me over now because I've thrown myself at you the moment you beckoned?"

"Shut up, *habibi*."

He closed his eyes and that was a bigger mistake because with him deprived of that sense, now all of his being was focused on her palming his erection. He grunted his assent, giving himself over to her curious fingers.

She wasn't urgent or greedy or fast now, but devastatingly thorough. The smack of her lips had him watching her again.

Pushing her hair away from her face in a gesture that was sensuality and innocence combined, she gave her full attention to the task of undoing him. The tip of her pink tongue stuck out between her teeth as she unzipped his trousers and then her fingers were sneaking under his boxers to fist his shaft with a soft, hungry growl that pinged along his length.

Breath hissed out of him in a guttural whisper, his hips automatically pumping into her hand like a schoolboy being touched for the first time. Her own mouth fell open on a soft gasp, calling his attention back to her.

Eyes drunk with passion, tongue licking her

lips, she watched him with an artless abandon that was as arousing as her slow, tentative strokes.

"You haven't done this much, have you?" he said, trying his damnedest to put brakes on a situation that had long been out of his control. From the moment he had seen her again at the nightclub, in fact. Wasn't that why he'd fought begging her for help?

Something almost like anger flashed in those gorgeous brown eyes. "Stop trying to pin me down, looking for reasons to stop," she whispered in a voice that was so husky that he felt a surge of all his possessive instincts.

Hair a mess around her face, the silky corset falling apart again to reveal small, high breasts with plump tips, and acres of smooth, golden-brown flesh...she looked like his darkest fantasy come true. He wanted no other man to hear her like this, or see her like this—messy and unraveled, and so tempting that his mouth was dry. He wanted no other man to know her like this.

A filthy curse exploded out of him when she rubbed her thumb over his sensitive tip, gathered up a droplet of liquid and brought it to her mouth. She rubbed it over her lower lip, all the while holding his gaze in a challenge that undid him.

The last of his honor evaporated. Or maybe he'd had enough of his own lies and half-truths. She was right. He'd started this, and as always, she'd risen to the challenge of his dare, proving that she was magnificent in a way he'd never previously understood.

Because now he could see the invisible scars life had left on her and how she still walked through it full of heart. A heart that was unwillingly beginning to fascinate him as much as her body did.

Holding his gaze, she licked that lower lip, even as she cupped her own breast with her free hand. In between her fingers, the dark pink nipple peaked, beckoning for his mouth.

Hands on her hips, he lifted her and reversed their positions until he was sitting back against the chaise and she was straddling him, his erection pressed up against her slick, hot sex.

Instantly, her spine moved in a sensuous ripple, mocking all the constraints he'd use to bind her. Head thrown back, the cut-open remnants of her dress baring her to her navel, she was the wildest thing Nasir had ever seen.

Wrapping the fingers of one hand around the back of her neck, he stroked his tongue into her mouth, even as he filled his other hand with her small yet perfectly lush breasts. She moved again until the width of his shaft notched against her core. Sensation skewered his spine and his body threatened to give out. He laved at her swollen lower lip, ran his palms all over her smooth back, the tight dip of her waist, reveling in the soft, raspy growls that seemed to escape her mouth every time he let her move a little. He touched her everywhere and it only inflamed his desire further. The more he had of her, the more he wanted.

"I have no condoms. But I swear to you I'm clean," he whispered against her throat.

"I'm on the pill," she said, whimpering as he bit down on the madly fluttering pulse. "Please, Nasir. No more teasing. I need you inside me. Now."

The sheer naked need in those words was the last thing to shatter his control. Taking his shaft in his hand, holding her still with one hand on her hip, he thrust into her inviting warmth in one long stroke.

His grunt sounded euphoric to his own ears. The tight clasp of her sex made lights explode behind his eyes in a kaleidoscope of sensations.

Sweat beading over his forehead, heart pounding loudly in his ears, he reveled in the tight sheath of her body. Without even moving, he was already close. He held back, determined to wring another climax out of her. He'd leave her so boneless with pleasure that she never thought of doing this with another man.

He was so far gone, so deep inside his own head, his senses so deeply entrenched in pleasure, that it took him several grasping breaths to realize that Yana had gone awfully still.

He opened his eyes to find her looking a little shocked, one lone tear streaking down her angular cheek. He closed his eyes and cursed himself for eternity. Even then, comprehension escaped him. In his hurry to relieve her pain, he took hold of her hips and jostled her slightly, and then heard her soft gasp.

Finally, the truth dawned on him, and with it came indescribable anger.

Of course, even in this, she would make a villain out of him. He'd hurt her, unknowingly, and he needn't have. "You and your childish games," he bit out, a gravelly bitterness coating his words. "How clever you must think you are, *habibi*. Is this some kind of revenge, then? Are you winning yet, Yana?"

When she reared back to look into his face, there was pain and want and a host of things he couldn't read. She nuzzled her face into his neck, dampness seeping from her skin to his. And then she licked at the hollow of his throat and clutched him harder with her arms and below with her sex and that, too, was a pleasurable torment.

All of her was a weapon and she wielded it with such innocence.

But buried deep inside her as he was, even his anger was only an irritating hum and a tight knot in his chest that he could easily ignore beneath the unparalleled sensation streaking through him as she adjusted herself. She moved as if she meant him to burrow deep inside her and never come out.

When he clutched her hips again, this time to gently pull her off him, she seemed to come back to herself. A half-growl, half-groan fell from her lips, and she was truly the wildest thing he had ever seen then.

"No, you're not going to leave me like this. Not again. Not anymore." One hand sinking into his hair, she tugged imperiously, as if she meant to own him. "Finish this." Without waiting for his response, she took his hands and brought them to her breasts.

Questions tore through his brain, even as fresh pleasure zigzagged through him. She was warm and soft, and with her hands on his shoulders, she undulated her spine in such an instinctive ripple that he was suddenly nearly all the way out of her slick clasp. Again and again, she wriggled her hips in a sinuous dance; figuring out her own rhythm and letting her use his body to seek out her pleasure was both a delight and a torment to him, and the slip-slide of their bodies created a symphony wholly their own.

She was trembling now, and Nasir stroked her, petted her, whispering nonsensical words into her skin, even as she gained momentum and confidence. Her rhythm was crude, a little erratic rather than smooth, and yet it was still the most erotic thing he'd ever known.

"At what point is this going to be less painful and more about pleasure?" she asked with a smile, and that husky voice pinged on his nerve endings. He laughed then, and he kissed her as if she was the most fragile, precious thing that had ever come to his hand. It wasn't that hard because she was the most fragile, the most achingly lovely, thing he had ever held.

Slowly, softly, he thrummed his fingers all over her body, noting when she leaned in to the touch, and when another soft gasp escaped her mouth, feeling when she ground down. A more natural rhythm built as he started thrusting up when she brought herself down. The slap of her thighs against his, the tight tug of her fingers in his hair, the erotic slide of her breasts against his chest made his spine burn with his approaching climax.

Holding her back from him, he lifted her breast to his mouth and sucked until he could tell her own need for climax chased her. Fingers, lips, words, caresses, tongue, teeth... He used everything in his arsenal with a ruthlessness he'd long ago given up to drive her to the edge again, even as he held back his own climax by the skin of his teeth.

And then she was shattering yet again, calling out his name, as if he was the benediction, and not her, and her sex was milking him.

Nasir pushed her down onto the chaise still shuddering, and instantly, she wrapped her legs around his hips, creating the perfect cradle for him to sink into. They could have done this a hundred times before and it couldn't have been as perfect. So right. So good.

He began with slow, deep thrusts, willing himself to enjoy this moment, even as selfish desire urged him to go faster, harder, to show her how needy he could get, to somehow mark her as she was doing him with such little effort. Hair billowing around her head, pupils blown up, her lush mouth trembling with explosive breaths, and his name on her lips…she took him straight over the cliff with her.

He came inside her, and it was the most explosive release he'd ever had. All he wanted was to do this over and over again. He wanted to make her fall apart again and again. He wanted to lose himself in her. He wanted to *keep* her. And the arrogant thought released a host of other thoughts.

What a grave blunder he had committed just because his ego refused to be perceived as the man who'd done her wrong. What else could this be except a predatory urge to conquer her anger and her distrust and her wildness and *her*, in essence? Where else would this lead but to her pain and more scars at his hand when their relationship inevitably ended? What could he do to avoid that? What choices were left to him?

He'd closed himself off to feeling the very thing she wanted out of life, because he had nothing to offer her. Especially now he knew that beneath the numerous masks she wore, she was as vulnerable as a baby bird.

Contrary to the confusion wrecking his mind, though, he gathered her soft, trembling body to him, buried his nose in her neck and whispered sweet nothings into her skin long after she fell asleep like the fragile, trusting, wonderful woman she'd always been.

CHAPTER ELEVEN

IN THE END, Nasir ended up carrying her to her bedroom, and Yana was sure a battalion of people had noticed her disheveled and thoroughly seduced state. Hiding her face in his neck, she thought she might have even heard Amina's loud, disgruntled huff at seeing her son parade about the castle with his virgin lover in his arms, like a dark sacrifice he was bringing back to his lair.

And that made her giggle uncontrollably. So much so that it skated the edge of hysteria. Nasir tapped her lightly on the cheek as he placed her on his bed.

"Care to share what's so funny?" he asked, locking her between his forearms, his torso leaning over her like a tantalizing shadow.

Yana writhed on the bed, loving the cool comfort of the sheets against her bare, overheated skin. The slick wetness between her legs coating her inner thighs and lower made itself known.

"I was trying to imagine how we must have looked to your mother."

His mouth twitched. "That's the last thing I need in my head right now." When she continued to smile, he ran his thumb over her lower lip. "Tell me."

"Like you were a beast bringing your virgin sacrifice to your lair."

He bopped the tip of her nose even though his jaw tightened. Still sore about that secret of hers, then.

"You have quite the imagination, *habibi*."

"You don't know the half of it," she said, desperate to tease him out of the dark mood.

He straightened and watched her. A sliver of moonlight illuminated his own features for her. *Just for her.* All sharp slashes and hard contours and even with that scar ruining his lovely mouth…he'd always struck her as the epitome of sex appeal.

But she tended to forget that he'd achieved it by living a whole other life before she'd even grown to adulthood. He was always going to be out of her reach, if she thought like that. If she sought to put him on that pedestal.

But he wasn't, by his own claim. He wasn't a statue, either, however much he claimed that. And with the open sides of his shirt flapping about, his hair ruffled and made unkempt by her fingers, his chest bearing the slight scratches from her nails, he was *so utterly hers* then that her breath stuck in her throat. Possibilities fluttered through her heart, bolstered by the soreness of her muscles and the tender ache between her legs.

"No, I don't know the half of it. Or you."

And with that pointed remark, he was walking away. When every inch of her wanted to run after him like a half-naked, lovesick wraith, ready to prostrate herself to keep her with him for the rest of the night, Yana rolled away to face the other side of the bed instead, a strange kind of lethargy stealing over her.

His anger was a familiar companion she'd lived with before. Could live with again. But she did an emotional check on herself like Mira had taught her and Nush to do.

All through that long walk across his vast castle—no, even before that, when he'd roared his climax in her ears and she'd hidden away that sound in some deep part of her psyche, to be taken out in private and examined again and again—she'd been trying to muster up some kind of regret.

Or anger, or shame or guilt or any number of darker emotions that she was used to drinking up like a toxic cocktail when she made bad decisions. Because he was her darkest weakness and deepest want, and when he'd beckoned a finger, she'd gone running, hadn't she? She was a pushover if ever she knew one.

But the bitterness of regrets, the acidic taste of failure, refused to come this time. Not with the sweet, pulsing ache between her thighs or the swollen sensitivity of her lips or the soreness of her muscles to distract her... Instead, she felt alive and thoroughly debauched and gloriously loved. Maybe she should listen to her body more often and refuse to poison it with negativity, she thought.

Burying her face in the pillow, she gave in to the languid smile that fought its way through. If she put the *shoulds and shouldn'ts* aside, it felt like fate or the universe or some inevitable course she'd set herself on through the years that it should be Nasir who ultimately destroyed her fear and distrust in herself. As if all the previous wrongs had led to this one right.

But that way also lay the trap of romanticizing not just the sex they'd had but also the entire episode, the entire evening. Attaching meaning and expectations to it when there were none. The whole evening had built to this moment—no, years of attraction and dislike and even shared grief had all led to tonight. A once-in-a-lifetime thing, a self-indulgent, luxurious experience, a reward for all the bad things about her old life she was shedding, enabling her to move on into her new life. Having sex with Nasir was not a mistake, but it wasn't a new road to explore, either. There, that explanation suited her. She hoped her silly heart got on the same train.

"Turn around, Yana."

She rolled onto her back to find Nasir kneeling on the bed. Had she been so deep inside her head that she hadn't even noticed that he hadn't actually left, he'd just gone into the bathroom?

Hands on her knees, he gently opened her. A cool, wet washcloth on her sex made her hiss out a deep sigh. It felt damned good and that, perversely, made her resentful. "Have you done this a lot, then?"

"What?"

"Ministered to virgins after debauching them?"

His laugh was a booming sound—gravelly, with no hint of actual humor. "Yes. The sacrifice will come next."

Her mouth twitched. She let out a long, shuddering exhale, so that he knew that she was merely tolerating him. The wet splash of the cloth as he chucked it back into the bathroom made her eyes pop open.

"Nasir, I can look after myself."

"Of course you can, *habibi*. I'm under no illusion about what you are capable of anymore. But indulge me, just this once."

With that terse dictate, he began to pull at the sad remains of the dress from around her tired limbs. With an efficiency that reminded her that he'd once been a journalist covering the most dangerous places in the world, he briskly gathered her hair, pulled her up and dressed her in a T-shirt of his.

"Underwear?"

"Nope," Yana answered without missing a beat.

"Better and better," he whispered at her temple and then retreated again.

Only then did she realize she hadn't felt an ounce of hesitation at giving him a straight answer. As if they were an old married couple, used to the small intimacies that made up the best parts of a relationship. She had this strange sense that this should've been awkward and sticky and messy, and yet, it had that ring of inevitability about it again.

"I think you should leave now," she said, trying to cut the strings of the parachute of her dreams before it flew away into some magical fairyland where the messy, volatile princess conquered her beast with the all-consuming power of her love.

"I think differently." He returned, dressed in loose pajama bottoms and nothing else. All of his tautly muscled chest and back with its myriad scars beckoned her.

Pure, irresistible temptation.

"Scoot over."

"I don't think we need a postmortem, Nasir. It happened. It was fantastic. Now we move on."

When she didn't give in to his ruthless demand, he gave her a playful shove to the middle of the bed, and by the time she'd recovered from her quick roll, he was sitting up next to her, with his fingers pushing her hair away from her face.

Under the guise of straightening herself under the rumpled sheet, Yana gave herself a moment to fight the inexorable urge to stay like that, with his fingers raking through her hair with a tenderness she'd craved for so long. She also wanted to push off the duvet, shrug off the T-shirt he'd put on her and arch up into his touch. To dig her fingers into his hair and bring that sinful mouth down to her breasts again. At the mere thought, her nipples tightened, sending tingles straight down somewhere else. It was a weird state of arousal and languidness, and it took all the willpower she had to not just give in to the moment. To not just give in to him.

Shrugging his hand away, she sat up.

"Who said anything about a postmortem?" His voice was silky-smooth but with a hard undertone to it. "Maybe I'm looking for a repeat. Maybe I'm the beast who's finally got his filthy hands on the virgin princess and would be cursed for the rest of his life if I let her go."

She sent him a shocked look—his narrative was perceptively close to the one in her own head.

What was real and what was made-up fantasy between them? What was attraction and interest on his part and what was just a bunch of baggage he wanted to be rid of, in order to right his mistakes? And worst of all, why was this intimacy so easy between them? Why did the dark quiet feel like it was weaving a spell around them?

"Why all the lies, Yana? Why make yourself out to be someone you're not?"

"So I'm suddenly more valuable now because

I still had my V card?" She combed her fingers through her hair, quickly braiding it to the side. "I thought you a better man than that."

"I have committed enough sins without adding that one to the list, *habibi*. It doesn't matter to me how many men you'd slept with. It does matter to me that you've created a certain image for yourself and today you've decided to reveal the real you."

"Ahh, gotcha. You're worried that I might think you're special because you're my first lover?"

He clasped her chin between his fingers, an angry frown turning his face dark. "My point is that you decided to keep lying to me, even to the last second. Maybe you thought this would all be a big laugh, proving me wrong about you. Maybe it's just a grand game to you. But I won't make the mistake of assuming that tonight meant nothing to you."

And you? Did tonight mean more than nothing to you?

"No, you'll just assume that I want more from you than this. Isn't that why you are here now— to set the record straight? To make sure I don't see some big, bright future together?"

"Yana—"

"And people say women are the illogical ones. I won't cling to you, Nasir. How can I make that clear to you?"

"Why is even having a conversation with you a fight?" He sighed, the back of his head hitting the headboard. "This talk was coming, even if we hadn't had sex tonight. I'm not a man who bears the weight of his guilt easily, even when it's justly deserved." His tone hinted at volumes of grief and loss that shut her up instantly. "I'm here to appease my own conscience, to cater to my own ego, to make sure I don't fall off the pedestal I tell myself and the world I stand on. Pick whichever of those you feel best applies."

She laughed then and he glanced at her—her eyes, her mouth, her neck—and desire danced there, more than just a burning ember.

A whole conflagration waited there. Just that one look and everything she'd buried deep inside her heart awakened. In that moment she adored him more than she ever had, more than she'd ever thought possible again.

Here was the man who'd always been able to laugh at his own weaknesses and faults and yet had still tried to do better.

"Amina is going to hate me all over again," she said, searching for a safer topic.

"That tactic won't work."

"We have decided that it's your fragile masculine ego that begs to be tended to. What else is there to talk about?"

"What else about you has been a lie?"

Yana looked at her tightly clasped fingers and loosened the grip.

He had no idea what he was offering her. How burdened and cut off and lost she'd felt in the past few months. How she hadn't realized that her stubbornness to do it right finally, to take charge of her life in a meaningful way, would nearly be her undoing.

She'd be even more beholden to him, but outside of the sex, she was beginning to believe that he cared a little about her. Even if only to right past wrongs.

"You know more about me than Diana knows, more than my grandfather did. More than even my sisters." It didn't even surprise her anymore that he was the one who'd ended up being the witness to all of her failures and flaws but also the one who'd see her strengths, who'd give her the validation that she shouldn't still need but longed for anyway.

"Yana—"

"If you're going to spend the rest of the night here, I propose we do something fun, at least."

When he grinned like the careless, charming rogue she'd known once, she shook her head. "Not that, you rogue."

"Ahh… What do you have in mind?"

"Since I've given you my virginity and my deepest secrets—" although there was something else she'd fight with her last breath from giving him this time "—I think a favor's fair."

Something about the naughty twinkle in her eyes, the sheer enthusiasm in her words, made Nasir want to kiss her all over again. Instead, he leaned back and gave a beleaguered sigh. "You've already robbed me blind, *habibi*. What else would you have of me? More importantly, I don't believe you've given me all your secrets." He grabbed a thick lock of hair and tugged until she arched up toward him like a bow and his mouth hovered over hers in a tempting tease. "I think you like keeping me hanging."

With a flourish that made him laugh, she pushed him away, then sat up cross-legged, shoulders straight, readying for battle. His T-shirt fell off one shoulder, baring silky-smooth skin and drowning her in it. Hair in the messy bun again, face scrubbed of makeup, she looked utterly different from the sophisticated, elegant Yana she'd been earlier at dinner.

Even more beautiful in his eyes, because this was the real version no one knew.

Maybe no man should ever see her again like that, his possessiveness crowed, joining in with the irrational crowd of voices rioting in his head.

No maybe about it, said the part of his brain glutted on endorphins.

She should be mine. Only mine, the deepest corner of his heart announced, aided by his arrogance.

And how he could bring it about danced vaguely at the back of his mind. A solution would tie a bow around two of his dilemmas.

"You can ask me whatever you want," she said, her nose held high as if she was granting him a favor, unaware of the scheming his libido and his brain were doing together, "and I'll do my best to give you a truthful answer."

"Wow, and you think you're not a hard-nosed businesswoman? I don't want the most truthful answer, Yana. I just want the truth."

She frowned. "I have a pretty big thing to ask of you, so fine."

"Where do you disappear to in the evenings after Zara goes to bed? The whole damned staff knows but won't tell me. Loyalty to Ms. Reddy and all that. I should fire Ahmed because I think he's the one heading up that rebellious campaign."

The easy humor of two minutes ago evaporated and a heart-twisting vulnerability shone in her eyes. "Don't fire anyone on my behalf."

"Then tell me what you're doing."

Yana knew he was only joking—his staff was his family, so she should keep this particular truth close to her heart. But that reckless, defiant part of her wanted to tell him and test him and…

"You're scaring me, *habibi*. And that has happened only twice in my entire life. What secret is so dark and deep that you look like I'm asking you for a piece of your soul?"

With one perceptive sentence, he'd disarmed her all over again. "It costs a piece of my soul to tell you."

"Let's make you feel better, then. What do you want from me in return?" he asked, knowing that in that moment, he'd give her anything she asked for. It was only the high of good sex, he told himself, but the claim felt hollow.

Her face glowed from within as she softly whispered, "I want to read the advanced copy of your next two novels."

His chest warmed at the childlike fascination that made her eyes glitter like priceless gems. "That's it?" he teased and then said, "Done." Pulling her to him, he kissed the tip of her nose. "Now, give it up, *habibi*."

Her chin lifted and a new kind of light shone from her. He was a writer but he had no words to describe the exquisite expression in her eyes. It was hope but brighter, shinier, more radiant.

"I'm writing a book. It's actually the second in a series and I think it's good. Like, really good. I also wrote a fantasy horror that's based on Indian mythology in the last few years. Thaata used to tell me all the scariest stories, you know? He used to say I was the only one among the three of us sisters who didn't scare easily." Pride he'd rarely seen danced in each word. She drew in a fast, shallow breath as if she couldn't stop talking now that she'd started. "I don't know if you've noticed but I had quite a rigorous discussion with your editor Samuel earlier tonight. I kinda ran the premise by him and he said he'd take a look at the book. How fantastic is that? Which reminds me that I should thank you for inviting me to today's gathering and—"

He laughed then and tackled her onto the bed until they were all tangled up in each other and the sheets, and there was nowhere she could escape to. He didn't remember the last time he had laughed so much, when listening to another person had brought him such joy, when he had felt such an overpowering rush of tenderness that he couldn't think straight.

"What's happening?" she said on a husky moan, when he covered her with his own body.

Ya, Allah, she fit so well against him—all soft curves and prickly edges and silky skin and sleek flesh and trembling thighs and tremulous moans. And those big, dazzling eyes reflecting everything she felt straight at him.

"You're so adorably sexy when you talk about your deepest dreams that I've been overcome by uncontrollable lust once again, *habibi*," he whispered at her ear and then followed it up with the filthiest words he could speak to her.

She blushed even though she didn't fully understand him and then those sleek legs converged around his back and she was lifting her hips up and Nasir ground his erection into her with no self-control.

A trail of damp kisses followed from her mouth, licking and nipping at his flesh. With one hand, she tugged up her T-shirt and through his silk pajama bottoms, he could feel the heat radiating off her sex. Pressing herself up against him, she writhed with a wanton pleasure that had his rock-hard length twitching.

"Please, Nasir. Now."

He took her mouth in a gentle kiss. "You will be sore, *habibi*. It might hurt a little."

"But after it passes, you'll make me scream with ecstasy, won't you? Twice at least."

And then without waiting for his response, she pushed down his pajamas and freed his shaft and then he was there at the center of her sex.

Reaching for a control he wasn't sure he possessed anymore, Nasir played with her soft core. Stroked her own wetness all over her until she was moaning his name like a symphony. Taking it slow with his fingers, letting her get used to him all over again. With all the skill he had, he teased her over and over and only when she began to fall apart, calling out his name, did he slide himself into her.

Slumbering heat built and built in his spine as he went slow and deep and shifted her pelvis up until he could hit a different spot and she was moaning that she couldn't go again. But he saw the need and greed in her beautiful face and he hit that spot over and over again, dragging his abdominal muscles over her sensitive nub and it was all an erotic tango that made his muscles clench and sweat bead all over his skin. When she screamed in pleasure and went over the edge again and buried her teeth in his pectorals, he followed her and fell apart along with her in a way he hadn't allowed himself in a long, long time.

After they'd showered, despite her complaints that she wanted to sleep, and he'd fed her pieces of crisp apples and cheese and nuts, she'd wrapped herself around him like a vine. When he'd tried to give her a little space, she crawled back to him and over him, limbs akimbo, aggressive and prickly even in sleep.

When he held her against his chest, she kept throwing her legs and arms around. And when he finally got her to settle down with a long, drugging kiss, she mumbled sleepily that she'd thought it would be like this, that she'd known that it would be him. That he was worth the wait.

Nasir thought his petrified heart might have cracked open at that vulnerable admission. And he wondered if stones could be turned back into men and even if they could, if they could relearn the most human thing to do again—to love.

Or if it was all too late for him. But he knew one thing about men; that they were selfish. He was one, too, and he knew he wouldn't give her up when she fit into his life so perfectly. Not ever.

CHAPTER TWELVE

THE NEXT SIX weeks were as close to paradise as even Yana's wildest dreams could have conjured them to be. It had felt unbelievable when she'd looked at her calendar that morning and realized there were only three weeks of her stay left, as per the contract she'd signed with Nasir. Of course, the contract had no meaning left between them except as a joke Nasir used when she'd ask something of him and he'd say she'd robbed him blind already.

Time seemed to rush at an indescribable speed the more she tried to double down on it. Or was it her grasp of time as a construct that was slipping because she'd never been happier, or for the first time in her life, that she was truly thriving and flourishing on all fronts?

She'd had to finish up the last of her modeling contracts already in place, so she'd done those. She and Nush had squealed with joy at learning recently that Mira was pregnant with twins—*twins*—and the sisters had managed a weekend for a much-needed girls get-together arranged by Mira's clearly besotted husband Aristos. *And* to top it all off, she was making good progress on the second book she was working on in her series.

It was still hard for her to trust Nasir with reading her work. Or maybe it was her insecurities? But she managed to reveal theoretical scenarios to him because his mind was a maze and he was the best at brainstorming. While it rankled him a little that she refused to share more, he always indulged her outlandish inquiries and they ended up discussing craft and the industry and research so often that Yana began to fall for him all over again.

Between quick one-day or overnight jaunts to different locations for a magazine ad shoot, a perfume ad and the opening of a new night club in Amsterdam, she'd spent the past few weeks soaking in the sun, swimming in the pool and wandering the woods with Zara in tow.

Nasir, to her shock, had shown up at the same hotels as she had for almost all of her work trips. To her unending delight, he was one of those people who'd been to every damn city in the world and always knew the best places to eat, knew the real history that books seemed to forget and then there were those glorious nights of passion and tenderness and more to explore between them. The best part was that she felt as if the trips were slowly bringing out the true explorer of life Nasir was at heart.

After that first night, they didn't try to label what was between them again or set an expiration date on it, and that was perfectly fine with Yana.

Clearly, he still wanted her with the same fervor and madness she felt. In this, finally, they were equals. They were lovers and confidants and shared all the ups and downs of loving and caring for a little girl.

She was living the life she'd once dreamed of and during those glorious moments where they were playing with Zara, or reading quietly together in the evening, or talking about her book, it felt like it was more than enough. At least that was what she told herself, trying her best to not give too much thought to the future.

Not confiding in her sisters when she wanted to share the real relationship she was finally having with Nasir, hurt her heart. But they would only ask about where it was all leading, out of pure concern for her, and then Caio and Aristos would be dragged into it, and she didn't want to force the issue when it was, in the end, all a precarious house of cards.

For now their *affair*—for want of a better word—still possessed that dreamy, magical, out-of-this-world quality to it and she was loath to disrupt it with talk of reality and future and stupid, silly organs getting far too involved when they should know better.

It was the same when they were at the castle, too—as if the whole scenario and the actors had truly emerged out of a dark fairy tale into a happy romance. She didn't know if the instructions not to mention it had come from Nasir.

She was only thankful that the staff and Ahmed and even Amina acted as if they didn't notice anything. Nasir's mother had been excessively, exactingly kind to her, and Yana had cautiously returned the courtesy because Amina seemed to finally realize how much Yana had loved her husband. How real her mourning of Izaz was.

But sometimes, Yana saw a calculating quality in the older woman's eyes and it unnerved her. She kept pointing out with a tone to her voice that Yana couldn't pin down, that Zara was flourishing, thriving, blooming, under the attention of the two adults she loved the most.

Especially since she must know that her son ended up back in his bedroom—which Yana still also occupied, every night without fail. Though Nasir left before dawn at the latest—immediately after sex sometimes—to return to the bedroom he'd used since she'd arrived.

Yana had initially found both injury and insult in his leaving right after sex until he'd explained to her, with that charmingly wicked smile of his, that inspiration for his next novel had been coming to him in waves around midnight, right after he'd made love to her. That if he didn't want to be ditched by his frustrated editor or his agent, he had to capitalize on it. And that he'd been making the trip back to her bedroom after his writing session, only to leave at dawn again because they didn't want to be caught together by his curious five-year-old.

Acting the seductress—a bad habit that Nasir demanded she'd better *not* give up because it made her say and do outrageous things just to provoke him, she'd prettily suggested to him that he'd better dedicate the book to her for her part in getting it done.

His reply had been, "I wouldn't want to shock my loyal readers with all that went into finishing the book, *habibi*. Those particular details are only for me to savor. Especially the time you decided you wanted to be on your knees."

She'd blushed so hard that her cheeks had burned. But she'd also been secretly glad—not because she believed sex with her had some magical writer's unblocking properties, but because, for the first time in years since she'd known him, Nasir genuinely looked relaxed. Content. Happy, even.

And she wanted to think at least some of that— a tiny, little part—was to do with her.

The summer sun had already started to set, immediately bringing a cool chill that particular evening as Yana hurriedly packed up their picnic supplies. Especially since they'd ventured farther than the boundary of the woods they usually stuck to. It was her own fault for giving in to Zara's continued request for more playtime. Between keeping up with her and her own flagging energy, Yana hadn't checked the time.

Yana pushed to her knees and lugged the heavy tote bag—Zara had to bring all the rocks she'd collected today, onto her shoulder just as the little girl, in her hurry, slipped over something and fell facedown into the knee-high grass.

Dropping the bag where she stood, she rushed to Zara. The five-year-old's cry—a sudden, spiraling wail—told Yana it was more shock and fear than real pain. Fighting the worry in her head, she squatted on the floor and gently pulled Zara into her lap.

The little girl attached her arms to Yana's neck with a hiccupping cry, without letting her check her face. Sighing, and loosening her arms so that she didn't communicate her own fear to her, Yana rocked from side to side even as she whispered that Zara was okay. When Zara finally let her look at the small cut on her cheek, Yana set about dealing with it.

She wasn't sure how long it took, when suddenly Yana noted that complete darkness had fallen. With the forested area at her back, and the castle at least a mile in the opposite way, it would be easy to get lost without light.

Pushing onto her feet, she talked Zara into wrapping her arms around her neck and her legs around her back like a little baby monkey they'd seen on a nature show not a few days ago, clinging to its mother.

Wiping her tears on Yana's T-shirt, Zara instantly cheered up.

Turning around with her lightweight baggage, Yana walked back to where she'd dropped the tote. She found her cell phone and turned on the flashlight, although there was no signal to call Nasir this far out. The sky was a dark canopy of stars she'd rarely seen and she stopped several times to show Zara this star and that constellation.

Her arms and legs hurt from all the day's exercise but soon, Yana could see the shadowed outline of the castle. She blew out a long breath, imagining herself in a hot bath with Nasir in it, too, hopefully, once they'd settled Zara into bed. It was a ritual she hadn't planned on getting involved in and yet, had been roped into when Zara had begged that they both read her a story and tuck her in for the night. As if even the little girl could sense the current of happiness between the adults who adored her.

Now, with her departure rushing at her with every day that passed, the ritual and so many more like that had gained weight and gravitas. Yana didn't want to leave. There, she'd admitted it to herself. For the first time in her life, she was happy and content and…she felt like she belonged here. Like the castle walls themselves were imbued with her very joy.

"Where the hell have you been?" Nasir's question tugged her into the present with a firm jerk.

Taken aback by his tone, Yana stared at him.

"Do you know how worried I've been? It's dark and you weren't at your usual spot."

"I didn't notice the time and then Zara—"

"You should know better than to venture out so far and for so long after sunset," he said, plucking Zara from her arms into his. "That was careless of you, Yana."

Yana froze, struck by the criticism in his voice. But whatever defense she wanted to provide was drowned out when the entire staff came toward the high entrance from all directions surrounding the courtyard, clear relief on their faces. And then she was being tugged inside, by Amina of all people, who checked her arms and legs and worried over her dirty T-shirt and shorts, and all through it Yana kept looking at him, but Nasir wouldn't meet her eyes.

Suddenly, Yana felt as if she'd been permanently pushed into a cold, dark place, shunned from all light. All her doubts about how she'd leave when the time came turned into something else.

Finally, they were all in the full foyer illuminated by one of those blasted chandeliers with a million little lights and her gaze fell on the small cut on Zara's cheek just as everyone else's did.

"You're hurt, Zara," Nasir's voice cut through the commotion around them, like a knife slicing through. And Yana heard it then—his fear. Saw the tension carved into his face. The sweat that had gathered over his brow.

"I didn't listen to Yana Auntie, Papa," Zara said, scrunching her face up. "She told me not to go too fast but I thought I saw a dragonfly and then I fell over." Her thick curls dancing around her face, she drew in a long breath. "It doesn't hurt, Papa," Zara piped up, looking for Yana among the crowd that surrounded her. "Yana Auntie alweady cleaned it and put a gel on it. She said I get a medal because I only cwied for thwee and a half minutes. She said I was so bwave when she cleaned it that I could eat chocolate cake in the morning. Can I have chocolate cake for bweakfast, Papa?"

The tension dissipated from Nasir's face and he pressed a kiss to Zara's temple. "Yes, pumpkin. You can have anything you want for breakfast."

"Will you and Yana Auntie wead me two stories each tonight, Papa? Since I fell and hurt myself?"

Nasir laughed and hugged his daughter tight. "Manipulative little thing, aren't you?" When Zara frowned and pushed out that lower lip she deployed like a weapon, he hurriedly added, "Yes, two stories each, Zuzu baby. After that you have to sleep, yeah? And then…" He looked up over Zara's head and met Yana's eyes. "I have a very important thing to do."

"What, Papa?"

"Eating crow, baby," he said with a sudden, heart-wrenching smile aimed straight at her heart. Zara pounded him with more questions and he went on to elaborate that her papa was a blockhead who forgot his manners when he was upset. And he had been upset, he told Zara and an arrested Yana, at the thought that his two bestest, most favorite girls in the world might have been lost and hurt in the forest in the dark.

Yana's heart swelled in her chest, overflowing with emotion. And she knew, just knew, that she was going to leave pieces of herself behind when she left.

They ended up spending more than two hours not only reading to Zara but also watching some anime with her. Even though, for the first time in his life, Nasir wanted his little energy bunny to fall asleep fast.

In the end, he left Zara and Yana cuddling in

Zara's bed, both of them suddenly fast asleep together.

He went back to his own bedroom, made some quick arrangements in the bathroom, changed into pajamas and waited. He couldn't blame her if she didn't join him tonight, could he? He'd been so eager to criticize and blame her for a small hurt Zara had received.

He pushed a hand through his hair and tugged at it roughly. Of course, five-year-olds got hurt all the time. Why hadn't he controlled himself better? And now here he was, once again, wondering if he'd hurt her.

He'd worn down the carpet when the connecting door finally opened and Yana came in, locking it behind her.

They stared at each other—her expression wary as she watched him, and he...he didn't know what he looked like. Only that he wanted to make more than simple amends. Reaching for her, he took her hand in his and tugged her into the bathroom.

Her eyes widened as she saw the full bath he'd filled with her favorite lavender oil and scattered with rose petals, and the lit candles and the bottle of wine with a glass, waiting on the rim. "Nasir—"

Forestalling her argument or a justly deserved complaint, he said quietly but firmly, "Raise your arms."

He was more than surprised when she complied. Tugging her T-shirt off, he gathered her hair and gently tied it into a knot at the top of her head, like he'd seen her do. Then he stripped her of her bra and shorts and panties.

Eyes wide in her face like a gazelle, she stood there, utterly naked.

"Into the tub," he said gruffly, before his desire overtook his common sense.

She complied silently. Again.

He watched with sheer fascination that apparently refused to even simmer down into something manageable, as her limbs disappeared beneath the water and she threw her head back with a soft moan.

He swallowed when he caught sight of her tight nipples playing peekaboo under a rose petal. Needing to give himself something to do, he uncorked the wine and poured it into the glass.

She took it from him wordlessly and then took a sip. She murmured appreciatively and she wriggled her shoulders as if to dislodge a knot there. His guilt intensified. "Once you get out of the bath, I'll work those kinks out of your shoulders," he said, wriggling his fingers at her.

"No, thank you," she said, not opening her eyes. "Especially if your massage skills are no better than your daughter's."

"Try me and then pass judgment, *habibi*."

Another exhale left her. "Thank you for this.

It was exactly what I needed at the end of a long day."

Seating himself at the edge, he watched the overhead lights play with the angles of her face. "I shouldn't have snapped at you when you got back. I was worried, terrified, that you both were hurt. I… I was suddenly reminded of everything I once lost…"

"It's okay, Nasir," she said, lightly tapping her fingers over the back of his hand and then retreating. "I got that from your face. But just so you know, Zara's five and she's going to get hurt sometimes. Under my supervision or someone else's."

"I know that, in here," he said, pointing toward his head. "And the amazing thing is she knows that, too, doesn't she? She's completely fearless with you. But I do worry about her, Yana. All the time. Especially since I've already messed up with her once, so badly."

Opening her eyes, Yana watched him with that silent gaze. Asking questions without asking them. Waiting for him to reveal his darkest fears.

"I never planned to be a father, Yana. And yet, ever since I held her that first day, I've loved her. I know I can't keep her wrapped up in cotton wool, surrounded by staff who watch her twenty-four hours a day."

"You can't. And as much as you'll hate me for saying this, she'll be six in three months. She needs kids of her own age to play with, Nasir, to learn social skills, to learn boundaries. Even if you decide to homeschool her. You can't keep yourself shut out from the rest of the world and also be a good father to her. Kids need to learn about the world, and Zara's a pretty social kid."

"I don't hate you for saying it. In fact, I..." He swallowed the words, loath to unburden himself to her when he hadn't broached the topic in his head yet with her. He was aware of days dwindling at a rapid rate, of her looming departure. And yet, he held out. Told himself he and Zara would manage. Told himself that Yana would return to her normal life and yet they would still be able to resume their affair and fall into some kind of a sticking pattern, long distance.

He'd never been an indecisive man before in his entire life and he hated that he was waiting for time or something else to decide for him when he'd never done that. The certainty of time passing and the uncertainty of his own plans were eating through him.

He looked up and met her gaze. "I hope you won't ever stop saying that, Yana."

"Saying what?"

"What you think is right for Zara. Even if you're afraid that I'll get all grumpy and grouchy with you."

"I'm not afraid of you, you beast," she said teasingly, splashing water on him.

He went to his knees and then cradled her neck. Pressing his mouth to her temple, he whispered, "Even after you've left here?"

She grabbed his forearm. "I won't," she whispered earnestly and he heard the promise in it.

"Am I forgiven, then?" he said, trailing his mouth to the shell of her ear.

Her questing hands went straight to his erection. She palmed him and Nasir forgot all about the world outside. "Only if you get into the bath with me."

That was an invitation he could never resist.

CHAPTER THIRTEEN

YANA'S THREE MONTHS were up as if someone had taken the hourglass and shaken it up to make time go faster. She had an assignment in New York, then she was going to visit her mother in California and then return to be with Mira for almost a month before the twins were born. Of course, she'd promised Zara that she'd visit her, too, whenever possible in the midst of her hectic schedule. And she'd meant it. For once, everything in her life had the patina of normality and it left her feeling out of sorts.

She was at peace with herself, with where she was going in her life. She'd continue to pick up small contracts here and there until something definite came up in her literary career. Just thinking about that sent a ripple of excitement through her.

In the meantime, she had two sisters she adored and two billionaire brothers-in-law who were forever inviting her to visit and meant it. And Yana decided she would. She'd worked in one way or another since she'd been sixteen and she would take it easier now that she was already at a cross-roads.

She'd kept waiting for the bubble that Nasir and she seemed to live in to break, for reality or some other ugly life thing to fracture their almost fantastical happiness. When it happened, it did so because, once again, she couldn't help herself bringing up the past.

Because the seeds of the future had already been sown somewhere in the past and, in the end, because she'd realized the truth that had never changed.

That final day, Amina and Ahmed had taken Zara to meet Amina's sister in London, leaving Yana and Nasir behind. At his dictate, she'd learned later. To make it easier on Zara when Yana left the castle, but she wondered if he thought she'd also cause a scene.

Dread and something else curled around Yana's chest. She'd miss Zara with all of her being. She'd miss the staff, Ahmed's gentle care, Huma picking at her for ideas and even Amina, who'd thawed so greatly that she'd once said Yana was the daughter she'd never had. As skeptical as she'd wanted to feel, she'd thought the older woman had actually meant it.

As if her dark fairy-tale romance had to continue the theme, a great storm darkened the skies that last evening, chasing her and Nasir indoors.

As if someone had set a background score, a hum of anxiety had thrummed through her all day.

As usual, Nasir and she ate together, then worked for a little while on their respective laptops in the great big library in quiet, comfortable silence. He put the gramophone player on, and she stood up to stretch and suddenly, he was behind her, clasping his arms around her and leading her in a slow, sensuous tango around the room.

She had no idea how long they danced like that. How long they stayed silent even as their bodies communicated freely and easily and effortlessly. In her three-inch heels, she was at perfect height for the V of her thighs to feel his thick erection. She'd gone braless and her nipples felt deliciously tormented pressed up into points against his hard chest.

He tilted her chin up with insistent fingers and Yana read his raw desire as easily as she could hear the thundering pulse of her heartbeat in her ears.

She went with a willing wantonness as he pressed her upper body over a centuries-old side table full of crystal decanters and expensive candlesticks. She moaned like a brazen seductress when he pulled up the hem of the icy-blue cocktail dress she'd worn for him because he'd whispered once when he'd been deep inside her that he loved seeing her in it. She turned her head and let him see her greedy abandon with an eager push of her hips when he tested her damp readiness. She slammed her palm onto the dark wood when he thrust into her with one long, deep stroke. The decanters and the candlesticks rattled, the table hit the wall with a rhythmic thud and the entire castle felt like it was standing witness to them, and she wondered just who was seducing and who was surrendering.

And then she realized it didn't matter anymore.

Her breath came in sharp pants and shallow gulps when his thrusts began to gather speed, but suddenly *lost* that finesse. Then his fingers were at her core, and his mouth was at her neck and he was demanding she come for him and he was telling her she was the sexiest thing he'd ever beheld and he was all over her and around her. The clever, wicked man that he was, he hit the exact spot where she could see glorious stars and soon, she was climaxing so hard that she thought she might never come back together in the same way ever again.

Yana felt undone, unraveled, as if he'd wrested away parts of her. Her legs wobbled when he helped her straighten and she thought he was on shaky legs, too. She turned and smiled and then he was kissing her and telling her what a good, quiet, biddable lover she was and she was thumping him in his chest with her fist because he was deliberately provoking her all over again before he kissed her.

She had no words to describe the tender reverence with which his lips touched her. How they said so much that he couldn't or wouldn't say. She buried her face in his neck and let herself drown in the delicious scent of the man.

They stood like that, while the storm raged outside the castle, and Yana wondered at how perfectly it mirrored everything that was happening inside her.

"Come back to me, *habibi*."

"I'm here," she said and yet she felt like parts of her were going to stay behind forever with him. "I'm leaving tomorrow morning."

"I know."

"Thank you for giving me tonight. With you. With just you."

"You think it was a favor to you? It was a selfish man's selfish desire. To have you all to himself for one final night."

"Then for the first time in our lives, I think we're in agreement," she said, forcing a humor she didn't feel. "I'll return whenever I can."

"I know."

"I'll call Zara every day."

"I know."

"I'll let you know when you can drop her off with me. Mira would love to see her, too. And Aristos. And Nush and Caio. I want Zara to meet them all. I want her to think of them as her family, too."

"You're very generous, *habibi*, and Zara is lucky to have you."

"Are you mocking me?" she asked.

"Do I dare?"

She looked up and ran her fingers over the scar almost obsessively and then pulled back. "I'm sorry."

"You're welcome to touch me anywhere, Yana. Even the scar. I don't mind."

"I know," she said this time, and he smiled, and she smiled back, and it was a moment of perfect communion.

Age had only made him more handsome, more distinguished. Laugh lines crinkled out at his eyes even as grief and loss had permanently etched themselves onto those stern features.

It came to her then how much he'd changed after the incident that had given him those scars, how a shroud of grief had hung around him. With her usual foolish naiveté and a reckless urgency because it had pained her to see him like that, she'd not only trodden on his raw, wounded emotions but also declared shamelessly that she was in love with him and that he belonged to her.

God, had she ever read a situation so badly?

Whatever had happened on that trip had changed him—inside and out. Now she wished she'd asked him about it instead of throwing herself at him, that she'd kept a safe space for him like he'd done for her. Like he was doing for her again now.

But as much as she tried, she couldn't be mad at herself for her grand avowal of love back then. She'd sensed something was wrong with him and with her usual all-guns-blazing attitude had desperately wanted to fix it for him. She'd thought herself enough to fix him.

But it didn't really have anything to do with whether she'd been enough or not. Something else had happened to him on that trip. Now she realized it, and like that saying, the truth did set her free.

It was life affirming to have someone who loved you by your side when you went through hard times. But in the end, one had to save oneself. One had to decide to live and love despite the pain and pitfalls life threw at you.

"Who did you lose on that trip when you came back with all these scars?" she asked, twisting her fingers so that they cast shadows on his white shirt when what she wanted to do was look into his eyes and see the answer for herself.

The atmosphere dropped to frost instantly even though he was warm around her.

She closed her eyes, cursing her impulsivity. Just because he'd found her good enough for an affair didn't mean they were going to exchange every painful secret. But to her surprise, he answered.

"A photographer I'd been training for a while. Fatima was—" a small smile painted his mouth "—young, and brash and defiant and wanted to change the world for the better. I brought her with me on an assignment I shouldn't have. She died in my arms."

"You loved her," Yana said, stating the fact rather than asking him, the final puzzle pieces that made up Nasir suddenly falling into place.

"I did. And I should've done a better job of protecting her. I was more experienced than her. I should've done a better risk analysis—"

"Weren't you yourself hurt by the blast?"

"Yes, but—"

She laughed then and it was an empty, mocking sound that rivaled the storm's fierceness. "How heavy your ego must be, Nasir. Don't your head and your shoulders and your back hurt from the weight of it?"

"You don't understand—"

"No, I understand it perfectly. I see it, finally. I see all of you, too," she said, throwing his words back at him. "I see now why you shut me down with such brutal cruelty."

Suddenly, his marriage to Jacqueline—which had had disaster written all over it from the beginning—his withdrawal from the world, from his first career, from his father, and even from her, made complete sense now. It was what Izaz had meant when he'd said his son was lost.

After that trip he'd seemed colder, harder, flatter even, with none of those soft edges that added such charm to his incisive brilliance, none of the quirks and awareness that had made him…larger than life. Her own naive stupidity had been but a cinder in the sacrificial pyre he'd already built for himself.

"You don't understand how terrible it is to have someone you love die in your arms. How utterly powerless you feel. The memory itself would haunt you forever."

His words were a death sentence to her poor heart's tentative whispers. But she was damned if she let him believe he was right. That somehow, he had to live through this punishment, forever alone. "No, I haven't lived through that exact scenario. But I know about loss and grief and… screaming at the universe for just one last chance. One do-over. I'd give anything to have one last minute with Thaata, to tell him that I was sorry, that I finally see what he'd been trying to do all along. That I loved him so much."

Nasir took her stiff hand in his and clasped their fingers tight. But still, Yana wasn't done. She was furious, actually, on behalf of herself and Jacqueline and the woman he'd lost. Not to mention Zara.

"I'm sure Fatima would have loved to know,"

she said, crossing all lines, venturing once again into that forbidden zone, her reckless tongue bashing out truths he'd hate to hear, "that her death has been conveniently reduced to the reason you have turned away from living a full life. And you dare call me a coward?"

"It's not cowardice if I want to leave emotions out of my decisions. Not that I succeeded with you, I admit."

"Ha! Then why hate me for so long?"

"Because you were right. I lost the battle against myself over you long ago. Don't you see how that must have driven Jacqueline crazy? My dislike for you was far more potent than anything I ever felt for her. It didn't matter that I told myself to stay well clear of you. You were always there at the periphery of my life, teasing and taunting me. I wish I'd just admitted defeat sooner. You and I both know we were heading here, one way or the other, for years now, Yana."

"Because you were so sure that I'd throw myself at you again?"

A pithy curse was his aggrieved response. "Because as much as I fought it, a few days ago, a few months ago, a few years ago, when you were Jacqueline's maid of honor, even when you were my nineteen-year-old stepsister with the body of a goddess and the innocence of a locked-up princess, I was attracted to you. I wanted you all along. You have no idea how close I came to taking what you offered all those years ago. How I wanted to use you to bury my grief, to relieve the guilt I felt about Fatima."

"And why would that have been so wrong? Why do you talk of it as if it fills you with horror to even think it? I was only nineteen, yes. But how do you measure adulthood? How dare you take away my agency? I'd been through loss and neglect and rebellion and wrong influences and bad parenting...so much already. You were a good thing in my life. Loving you was a light in a place of shadows and mistakes and I'll never ever regret it."

"Don't, *habibi*."

"I don't want to play games or fantasies, Nasir. In this, I've never been able to dupe even myself."

His forehead pressed against hers, his exhale exploding over her lips, washing away her fears all over again. His hands cupped her shoulders and held her to him, hard and tight. The contact was nonsexual, seeking and giving comfort, and yet she felt it pass down through limb after limb, vein after vein, reaching the deepest corners of her and staying there. Rooting her to the moment, to the man, to herself.

Bringing her back full circle to her own truth. That she still loved him. That she'd loved him for all the yesterdays of her life and that she'd love him for all the tomorrows yet to come.

And this time her love didn't feel wrong or bad

or forbidden or immature or selfish or demanding. It simply sat in her heart, fitting in, settling into place. It felt like coming home.

"You're punishing yourself for a mistake you didn't even commit. With me and with Fatima."

"I'd have discarded you afterward. I had nothing to give you back for your declaration of love, Yana. I'd have simply used you."

"And now?" she asked, even though she'd promised herself she wouldn't go there.

"And now, I still have nothing to give you." He held her gaze, and she saw it coming before he said, "Except marriage."

She jerked back. "What?"

"Marry me, Yana. I'll give you every happiness that I can, make every dream of yours come true. Marry me because Zara needs you and I need you. Marry me so that you never have to say goodbye to us again. Admit it. It's killing you to leave. Admit that you're happy here with us."

Tears and smiles came at her together as she gazed at him. She couldn't lie to him now, even if she wanted to. Because it was her most sacred truth. "I've been happy here. Happier than I've ever been in my life. And yes, it's killing me to leave you. The thought of coming back as just a friend into your life, of not calling this castle home, kills me. The thought of not seeing you and Zara for months on end...kills me."

"Then stay and marry me. Make a life with

me." He took her mouth in a hard kiss, and she felt herself melting. Falling. Weakening. But she had to remain strong against temptation. "Stay, *habibi*, and I'll be yours in all the ways that matter."

"No, you'll be mine under conditions and caveats." Regretful tears drew paths down her cheeks. "You're still trying to pin me down. To take everything from me without giving me anything in return."

He flinched, and her chest felt like it would cave in. Because she knew he was standing there, with one foot on the precipice, ready to fall with her, but he just wouldn't take that last step.

"Only you could make me consider marriage again after the nightmare with Jacqueline. Why can't you see that?"

"I don't want the little crumbs you can manage. I don't want anything from you," she said, trying to cover up the thundering of her thudding heart and rolling belly with a small smile. Who'd have guessed that her teen fantasy coming true would be such a horror in real life? Who knew she'd walk away when her deepest dream was finally within her reach? "Because whether you admit it or not, you're already mine. You've always been mine, by your own admission. I've owned you for a long time and I just didn't know it."

She felt free then. Free of fears and shackles and incessant demands and made-up rules. Because her love for him was a simple truth. Like the sun rose in the east. Like the storm that was raging outside but would leave the world renewed come tomorrow. Like the pain that was crashing through her right now but would settle into another scar in the months and years to come.

What she refused to do was to twist herself inside out ever again, with the foolish hope that she'd finally be loved the way she deserved to be. Not even for Zara or for him.

She clasped his cheek then and licked into his mouth. The taste of mint exploded in her mouth, fusing with her very cells. She let her hands roam the broad chest, the tapered waist, the hard planes of his back; she snuck under his shirt and traced all of his scars and…then she kissed him all over again, hoping it would last her at least until the dark dawn and the long day ahead.

"Goodbye, Nasir."

CHAPTER FOURTEEN

NASIR FOUND HER at a fashion show in Athens, Greece. He'd followed her there after learning, from his mother of all people, that she was with her sister Mira, who'd just given birth to twins.

It had been four months since she'd left.

He hadn't called her or texted her or even snuck a glance at her as she talked to Zara on a video call, stubborn and hardheaded to the end. But thoughts of her consumed his every waking and sleeping moment.

His bed felt cold and empty. His life felt colorless. His words had dried up again as had his imagination. He'd thought of a million questions he'd never asked her and wondered at her answers. That a lifetime wasn't enough for her to surprise him and delight him and annoy him and bring him to his knees again and again. And he was beginning to think it wasn't a bad idea to be on his knees for the woman he clearly adored.

And she, apparently finally wising up to what an extraordinary, incredible woman she was, didn't even steal a glance at him. Even his mother got screen time. As did Ahmed and Huma and his staff. Never a question or a comment about him or for him since she'd left them.

Not Zara. Never Zara.

Just him. She'd left him because he'd been a coward. And in one of those petty moments, Nasir found himself envious of his own six-year-old for the generous, lavish, unconditional love she got from her Yana Auntie.

All he'd wanted to do for weeks was storm through her brother-in-law Aristos Carides's lavish mansion like a bull on steroids, making claims and commitments that made him come out in a full sweat, and announce to anyone and the world and her, especially, that she was his.

He wondered yet again how long their red-hot affair would have lasted if he hadn't brought up marriage. Clever and perceptive as she was, she'd seen it for what it was—another contract he'd use to bind her to him, without opening his heart. Without actually committing to anything. Without giving her, the glorious creature she was, her due.

Now he was ashamed of how he'd attempted to manipulate her, even if he hadn't done it on purpose. Dangling the mirage of a dream as if it was some prize she would leap at.

Even though she'd made it clear that she wanted all the fireworks and passion and roller coaster of true love. Finally, it was the thought of another man giving her what he'd refused to that had spurred him into action. The thought of spending the rest of his life wondering where she was, who she was bestowing that warmth of hers on, felt scarier than the risk of opening his scarred heart to her, hoping she wouldn't deal it a death blow.

So here he was in Athens at a fashion show, the buzz that it was Yana Reddy's last show—another fact he hadn't been privy to because she wasn't talking to him, letting himself be photographed by media and paparazzi, giving rise to all kinds of speculation just so he could have one glimpse of her.

He wanted to see her shine and dazzle and sizzle. He wanted to be a part of her dreams coming gloriously true.

Whatever Nasir had imagined about how she'd look when she strutted onto the catwalk had nothing on the reality. The music, the crowd's energy and the sensual beauty of each model highlighted by carefully orchestrated lights and makeup and music…it was meant to bamboozle the audience.

Having been to a few shows in his twenties, and the couple of shows he'd been to during Yana's stay at the castle, he knew how this worked. And yet, when Yana walked onto the stage—the last of the models to do so—in the French designer's magnum opus: a glittery, rainbow-colored pantsuit, he was captivated anew.

Without a bra, the lapels of the jacket were stuck to her skin, baring most of her breasts, and she looked like a queen.

No, she was his prickly, fierce princess. And he'd been stupid to turn away from the best thing that had ever happened to him. To turn away from the incandescence of Yana's love. A coward, as she'd called him.

But there was no turning back now, because she'd brought him back to life.

He was bemoaning his habit of not drinking alcohol when the doors to the penthouse suite of the hotel opened and she stepped inside.

Smoky eyes and a pale glossy lipstick and shimmery glitter over her chest...she looked like a dark, alien goddess full of fire and passion. Her hair had been plastered to her scalp in some weird hairstyle that served to highlight the stark sharpness of her features. All angles and edges that were soothed by the promise held in that lush, wide mouth.

"I wondered if it was you I saw out there," she commented coolly, still standing there.

That explained her lack of surprise at seeing him in here now.

He nodded and swallowed and ran a hand

through his hair. She watched him, and he watched her.

"Not a fan of the after-parties?"

"Not really," she replied.

He stole a glance at his watch. He hadn't expected her for hours, not until dawn. Suddenly, he felt woefully unprepared for all the words he wanted—no, needed—to say, after a lifetime of employing them. "I thought you'd be there."

"You were the one who had me upgraded to this penthouse suite?"

He shrugged, waiting for her to slam the doors in his face and run off.

Instead, she walked into the suite, grabbed a bottle of water from the mini fridge and emptied it out. Then she opened another one, stood over the sink and poured it out over her hair and face. Her breath came in sharp, bracing spurts as the ice-cold water made goose bumps rise on her skin. "That's better. It feels as if all those lights and sounds are stuck to my skin."

He grabbed a hand towel from the bathroom and handed it to her.

She pressed her face into it and when she emerged from it, there was a resolve to her mouth that spelled his doom. "Will you tell me why you're here? Or can I go to sleep? I've been on my feet for eleven hours straight."

"Catch some rest. I'm not leaving until we've

talked," he finally said, following her to the sunken living room.

"I won't catch a wink knowing you're out here." She plopped onto one of the sofas and before she could stretch her legs onto the marble coffee table, he sat down. His hands were shaking when he took her foot in his hands, pulled the lethal-looking heels off and pressed his fingers into the arch.

"God, I've forgotten how good you are at that," she said, throwing her head back.

He repeated his actions with her other foot and an electric silence built around them.

"I've brought you good news," he admitted finally.

She sat up, pulled her feet from his lap. "What?"

"Samuel loves your book. He wants exclusive rights to it. This is big, Yana. You're going to be incredibly successful."

She threw herself at him so suddenly that his heart rushed into his ears. "Oh, my God! That's... awesome. I didn't... I can't tell you what it feels like to hear that. I..." Then she grinned, and there were tears in her eyes, but she rubbed them away quickly with the back of her hand. "Wait, of course you know how it feels. Thanks for telling me, Nasir. It means a lot. And it means even more that you came all this way to tell me."

"When Samuel told me, although I know he

shouldn't have, I begged him to let me be the bearer of good news."

"Why?" she asked, her mask falling, a sudden belligerence to that one word.

"I wanted to see your happiness. Your laughter. Your victory. Your passion. I wanted to see you, Yana." And before she could probe him further, he said, "Do you have an agent yet?"

"No. I do have a pile of increasingly promising rejections from two years ago. They'd gotten more personal, came with more feedback. But after the last round a year ago, I stalled. I worked a bit more on the book and rejigged some major plot stuff. With Diana's games and Thaata sick, my head wasn't in the right space to start querying all over again."

"Do you want me to recommend you to mine?"

"Why?"

"Why what?"

"Why would you recommend me? As a bonus for sleeping with you?" she said, half-laughing, half-mocking.

"You're never going to stop taunting me, are you?" he said, knowing he deserved it. "My agent is amazing and will do a fabulous job negotiating you the best contract with Samuel. Fair warning about Samuel as an editor, though. He's brilliant, but he might make you rip the book apart until you hate him, the book and yourself. Just stay…

strong and keep your vision for the book at the forefront, okay?"

Yana nodded, feeling a rush of joy and something almost like pride well up inside her. "You believe in me, then? That I could do this author thing?"

"Of course I believe in you," he said. "I'd love to read it and get a real sense of your work but I understand that you're nervous about letting people read it."

"Only you."

"Only me what?"

"It's only you that I'm twisted up about showing it to. I've given copies to both my sisters and brothers-in-law."

His jaw tightened. "May I ask why?"

She shrugged. "Before, I was afraid that you'd mock it. Mock me."

"You really painted me as a monster in your head, huh? And at every step, I added color to your rendering by confirming your worst impressions."

"I think it helped to paint you like that."

"Helped who, Yana? Because it's been eating me up."

"Me. It helped me. Every time I wanted to give in, admit defeat, throw in the towel, give up on myself, I'd get this image of you. I'd see you looking down at me full of anger and contempt and I'd tell myself, *no way*. No way am I going to give Nasir a chance to think less of me again. No way am I giving up. You were kinda like a fire under my butt."

"I'm horrified yet again by my cruelty toward you and how it has—"

She came to him then and clasped his cheeks with that bravery that colored her every action. "It was a good thing, Nasir."

"From which damned perspective, *habibi*?" he retorted, with an angry flush.

His fingers moved over her cheeks, soft and slow and reverent, as if he worried that he might mar her.

Yana leaned into his touch. "Even when I loathed you, you were a positive force in my life. I loved you. I wanted to be worthy of you. I—"

"You're worth a million versions of me, Yana. You're fiery and beautiful and worthier than a thousand sunrises and a thousand sunsets. Your heart is beauty and joy and life itself, *habibi*."

"You're making me cry."

"Par for the course, then," he said with a twinkle, and then he was kissing her, and every nip and lick was lust and reverence—two such opposing shades of the same sentiment. "I wanted to be the bearer of good news. Even that was selfish. Shall I tell you why I'm here, truly?"

"Yes. Now, Nasir. You've stripped me of all my roles and defenses. I can't be strong for too long. Tell me now. Please."

"The second piece of good news first. I had three pieces."

"There's more?" she said, wiping the back of her hand over her cheek with a vulnerability that squeezed his heart.

"I'd fill your days and nights with all the good news I can muster, *habibi*. But these are small in the scheme of things."

"Tell me, please."

"I have finally convinced Diana to enter rehab."

"What? How?" Yana pressed her hands to her mouth, disbelief a giant balloon in her chest. In all the months since she'd agreed terms with Nasir, she hadn't been able to make any progress with her mother, who had broken down and admitted that she had a problem but wanted no part of the solution. Yana had seen shades of a woman she'd once adored, and her resolve to help her had only intensified. But her efforts hadn't borne fruit yet.

He shrugged, as if it was indeed a small thing. "I tried to persuade her. Offered her incentives. Then I…" He rubbed a hand over his mouth, as if unsure of her reaction. "I sort of threatened her with being completely cut off from the rest of her family. I think it was a culmination of all three that finally brought success."

Yana laughed and then cried, feeling as if gravity had been stolen from under her. She knew how much he disliked her mother, how many bad memories were associated with her. How much he'd have hated even talking to her. And yet, he'd done it. For her peace of mind. For her happiness. She took his hands in hers. "I can't thank you enough."

"Now for the third piece," he announced, as if her gratitude made him uncomfortable.

"I'm ready," Yana said, her words a mere whisper compared to the loud thundering of her heart.

He placed a sheaf of papers on the coffee table in front of him. "These are custody papers. If you sign them, we'll share custody of Zara. You can have her for more than just a month. You can course correct me when I get it wrong. You and she can have each other without me in between."

Whatever high she'd been riding deflated and she crashed with a hard thud back into reality. "Why are you doing that?"

"Because I know how much you love her and I want you to have everything you want, Yana. I never want you to doubt your place in her life."

"Everything I want, Nasir?" she said, throwing his words back at him.

"Yes, everything. Including my heart, if you still want it."

Yana stared wordlessly.

"I'm in love with you, *habibi*." His gaze searched hers, studied her, seemed to devour her. Even now, confusion danced in his eyes and she wondered if he felt as untethered without her as she felt without him. "You're a sorceress, like in the dark magic tales of the old. Only instead of cursing me to a wretched existence, you brought me back to life. And if you'd let me, Yana—" now he was on his knees in front of her, his large hands on her thighs, his amber eyes glittering with such pride and devotion and love "—I'll show you how much I love you for the rest of our lives. Life without you is like words without emotions. You are my heart and soul, Yana. And I'm sorry it took me forever to realize that you were already and always mine. I was the one who had to grow worthy of you. Do you see?"

Tears filled and overflowed down her cheeks and he still couldn't stop talking. "And I'm so glad that you came to me, *habibi*. That you found me all over again. That you gave me another chance because now, finally, I see you and I'm so ready for the exquisite, fragile, prickly and precious thing that you are, love. I'm ready for all of you, sweetheart."

And then she was crying in earnest then, falling into his open, waiting arms, her shoulders shaking with these great, heaving sobs that seemed to rush out of her in a torrent, and Nasir just held her, feeling his own heart break and tear and come back together again, in some kind of loop, as if it could be made and unmade by her tears and her laughter and her joy and her promises.

It was a long while before she raised her head

and looked at him. Her eyes and nose were all pink and splotchy and she was so achingly beautiful that a flicker of fear flashed through him. "Do you want to marry me?" she asked.

"Yes. Now. Tomorrow. I… I've wasted enough time as it is."

Then she hid her face in his chest and held him so tight that he was reminded of his daughter's hugs. "Zara's already your child as much as she's mine. Just give me a chance, too, Yana," he said with growing alarm that she hadn't really given him an answer. "Give me a chance to do this right."

"And if I have lots of demands and conditions and negotiations?"

"Only if you agree to all of mine."

She was kissing him now and laughing at the arrogance creeping back into his words and she thought she loved him most like this. "And what are they?"

"You'll hire a wedding planner so you don't get stressed out. You'll sleep in my bed even before then. And if you want babies, *habibi*, then we'll have babies, even if it means I turn old and decrepit by the time they go to college. But the wedding will be in two weeks, Yana. No more. I won't wait, not even for your sisters. And it will happen on the castle grounds."

Yana couldn't help smiling at how he'd tried to make it sound like a request and utterly failed.

"The castle? The whole world will know where you live, then. Because I don't want a hush-hush affair, Nasir. I want a big bang of a wedding. I want the whole world to see you're mine. At least a thousand people."

His eyes widened and he flinched and then recovered fast. "Fine. It will be gloriously extravagant and beautiful and loud, just like you are. And afterward, we'll move to a different castle then and we'll have two different ceremonies and you can invite the whole damned world if you want."

He picked her up and carried her to the bedroom and Yana buried her face in his neck, her heart full of joy. "I'm all sweaty," she said, offering a token protest, but Nasir was already unbuttoning his shirt and she pushed his hands away because that was her job.

And then he was inside her and they were laughing and she was still crying a little and she wondered if one could explode out of sheer happiness.

Hours later, in the dark of the night, Yana sat up and looked at the man next to her, deep in sleep. She'd tired him out with her incessant demands, she thought with a smile. Switching on the night lamp, she pulled her clutch open and took out the letter she'd been keeping for just such a moment.

Her heart was full of love and happiness and courage and she wanted to greet her Thaata like this. Settled in her own skin. Finally, accepting all of herself. It was all he'd ever wanted of her.

To my wonderful Yana,
    You're funny and brave and loyal and contrary and argumentative and reckless and messy and I know you keep stealing my cigars. But my darling girl, did I ever tell you that you're perfect just as you are?
    You're loved so much, Yana, I promise you. Try to love yourself a little, too.
    Thaata

Tears filled her eyes and fell down her cheeks, the world blurring and reforming and blurring all over again. Yana pressed the note to her chest, laughing and crying and wishing she could hug her grandfather just one more time.

"Yana?" Alarm crossing his face, Nasir gathered her to him until she was drowning in the familiar scent of him. His mouth was at her temple, tension vibrating through him. "What's wrong, *habibi*? What happened?"

Yana showed him the letter and buried her face in his bare chest. "He loved me all along, Nasir. I gave him such a hard time, and still, he loved me."

"Of course, he did, my love. As I keep telling you, you're perfection indeed and your grandfather was a wise man to see it. As am I," he added with that exaggerated pride in his voice that he knew got her back up. "But if you still don't believe it, I'll tell you every hour. And show you every hour." His hands on her shoulders, he flipped them until she was straddling him and she could see those sparkling amber eyes fill with such tender reverence that she fell onto his chest.

"I love you, Nasir. And you're right. Let's get married. But I need at least a month, okay? Mira and Nush and Amina will kill me if I don't give us all enough time to look spectacular. Huma could design the dresses. Would you be mad if I wore black?"

And then while he grumbled about being thrown over for her sisters, she sat up, pressed her back to his chest and decided to call her sisters and share her good news.

When they arrived at Mira and Aristos's home a few weeks later with Zara in tow, Nasir made good on his promise to put up with her shenanigans whatever they comprised. He greeted Mira and Nush with that solemn look in his eyes, withstood Aristos's and Caio's inappropriately territorial questions about his feelings for Yana and then picked up her niece and nephew Eira and Eros in the cradle of both arms with a reverent care that only confirmed her own wishes to make their family bigger.

When he looked up and their eyes met and he

showed that he understood her most urgent and fervent wish with a raised brow and a hungry look, Yana knew that her life couldn't possibly get any better.

* * * * *

If you couldn't get enough of
An Innocent's Deal with the Devil,
then make sure you catch up with the other instalments of the
Billion-Dollar Fairy Tales trilogy,
Marriage Bargain with Her Brazilian Boss
and The Reason for His Wife's Return*!*

And why not explore these other stories by Tara Pammi?

Claiming His Bollywood Cinderella
The Surprise Bollywood Baby
The Playboy's "I Do" Deal
Returning for His Unknown Son
The Secret She Kept in Bollywood

Available now!